DEVIL'S HOLIDAY

DEVIL'S HOLIDAY

FRED MALLOY

CUTTING EDGE

ISBN-13: 978-1-957868-82-0

Published by
Cutting Edge Books
PO Box 8212
Calabasas, CA 91372
www.cuttingedgebooks.com

FRIDAY, DECEMBER 24th ...
3 : 0 0 P . M .

HE SAT on the side of the sagging bed, perspiring in beady droplets in his prized magenta checked shorts, the abrasive spreading harsh against his bare legs, wondering what in hell he was doing there. The liquor didn't give him the lift he needed, didn't surge through him with a wild, blinding change any longer. It just lay limp in the pit of his stomach and felt like an unhappy ulcer. That wasn't any good. If he didn't get a boot out of the stuff, he might as well climb on the wagon with the rest of the double A boys.

The late afternoon sun roasted the drawn shade behind him, shooting splinters of light through the jagged tears that you always find in the ancient roller blinds in every cheap motor court. He listened to the wishwishwish of the cars streaming past on the highway outside. It was soothing, and under any other circumstance, he could have dropped off to sleep. Desperately he wanted to sleep. He wanted it more than the other desire that awaited him in glossy, rayon step-ins, across the room. He didn't dare doze; that would be the crowning insult to the girl undressing in front of him. He stretched, absently patting her svelte curve, reaching across for the bottle with his other hand. He lifted it to his mouth and allowed a gurgle to slip inside.

He swallowed a little at a time, feeling the velvet fire of it course his throat. He looked up as the blonde crossed to him, sitting close to him, and he felt the heat of her that was a little warmer than the unbearable temperature of the room. She was

1

nude now, except for her pink, 20th century loin cloth. Her large, horn-rimmed glasses seemed strangely out of place, like a golf bag in the vestry.

She reached across him, pert, pointing breasts nuzzling his flesh, causing an intended quickening of the pulse.

"Any of that jug left for Baby?" she asked, grasping the bottle, taking an experienced swallow from the neck.

He found himself comparing this secretarial trollop with his wife. Actually, he decided, there was no comparison. They were altogether different types. Connie had so much poise, was so self-contained and sufficient unto herself. Even if she happened to open that door over there and catch him at it now, he doubted if she would allow any emotion to appear on her face. Maybe her right eyebrow would raise a little, but that would be all.

Again he wondered what he was doing in this little out-of-the-way motor court, with this little bitch he had picked up in the bar.

What was it that ruined a man's outlook occasionally? Making everything around him turn to gall and wormwood. When everything he had known and loved for years became meaningless, disintegrating under his touch and thought. When there must be a new excitement, a new thrill, a different conquest. Was it a vestigial trace of man's earliest ancestor, the wandering nomad? A strange terrain to conquer, an undiscovered horizon to claim for his own? Another slim torso to carve his initials on? He speculated on how many initials had been carved in this girl. Untold thousands, passing in review.

How often had he gone scampering off. Shutting his life with Connie away into another storeroom of his brain, bringing her out to admire and compare in moments of crisis. Like this one. Why did he have to consider himself such a daredevil explorer of the opposite sex? To put up a front with guys? To satisfy his ego? God knew that had been done often enough. And why had he always had such an easy time with women? His lean, hungry look, and that thatch of bright yellow hair, like a pool of sunlight on his head. And counting our assets, let's not forget that cynical half smile so religiously cultivated.

His drowsy daydream vanished as the girl leaned toward him, carmined lips seeking. He smiled to himself.

"What're you studyin' about, Kenny boy?" she cooed. "Isn't Mama showin' you a good time?"

He winced as he heard his right name. Under similar circumstances, he had always given another name, but this time, the girl happened to work in the office with him. He had violated one of his oldest maxims. Never get your bread and meat at the same market.

He let his hand slip down the furrow in her back, until the tips of his fingers just nipped under the single band of elastic of her lone garment. She snuggled closer, with a delightful wriggle. For the life of him, he couldn't remember her name.

"Sure, Hon, don't worry about me," he replied. He replaced Connie carefully into her special niche in his mind. "Here, let me show you what I mean."

He put his index finger under the nameless girl's chin, folding her in to him. He felt her breasts gently resisting the pressure of his chest. He strained tighter, and they melted together in warm heat. Ken bent his hungry mouth to hers, and she came on in slack lipped passion. His method of kissing easily surmounted her weakening defenses, if such there were. The heat of the day became greatly intensified inside the tiny room.

She arched under the passionate pressure, aiding him in divesting her of her sole protection from complete nudity. Finally, she drew away, soft chest heaving with frustrated desire.

"God, boy! Where'd you learn to kiss like that?" she asked, between gasps.

"Picked it up here and there."

"I'll bet. I can see you weren't hatched out on a rock."

"You wanted action, didn't you?"

"Yes, Lover. And I guess I got me the right boy."

"What are you bitching about?"

"Who's bitchin'? I'd just like to get my battery charged again, that's all."

She's ready as hell, he told himself, as he buried his face in her throat, gnawing at the warm, damp skin. She writhed against him, fumbling clumsily at him. Her breathing was hard, and she made tiny noises deep in her throat that he could feel against his teeth. Finally, her hand struggled up from his body, grasping his hair. Pulling his head down between her firm breasts.

"Stop it, you bad boy," she giggled. "You want to make hickies all over my neck? How would I look, going to work with my neck all black and blue?"

"Wear a turtle-neck sweater." His voice was muffled, coming from his new position.

"Silly."

She took a fresh grip of his hair, pulling his face up to hers. Kissing him, forcing him flat on the bed in a sudden burst of life. Ravishing him with her lips, nibbling at the ends of his ears. He struggled weakly against her passionate fury, his resistance, felt earlier, had vanished in ever diminishing circles.

A last surge of self-recrimination engulfed him.

What had become of his love for Connie? There had been a time when she had been the only vision in his mind. Tall, straight and dark. When they had become engaged, everyone had said what a lovely couple they made. Now, after five years of marriage—a short five years—there was nothing. True, they had been separated by nearly four years of war, but they were not alone in that. So had nearly everyone else. By all rights, that should have made their love even stronger.

Ken supposed that he still loved Connie, but not in the way he should. There was no tense excitement, waiting for the sight of her. Like back in school, when they had first started going steady. He could still remember the first time. But it was a dead thing now, and he found his thrills with others. Like this free tramp by his side.

He enjoyed the conquest, the sport of the chase. But now that was finished, he dreaded the consummation.

There was a price to pay for all this somewhere. And every woman who tendered you her utter caress, purchased a piece of your soul. You were the rampaging, high-stepping stallion, trampling God's buttercups willynilly in his garden. You never realized, until you entered the garden, how many gadflies there were.

You're never alone after someone has a piece of your soul.

"What the hell, Ken," he told himself, "you're snappin' your wig."

He looked up at the girl, nude, except for the ridiculous glasses, running her eager fingers over his body. He reached up lazily, removing her spectacles, giving them a little flip into the hammock at the end of the bed formed by the crumpled spread.

Her eyes looked wide and frightened, her face reflecting utter vacancy without the glasses. Twin, red blotches flamed on each side of her nose from the steamy pressure.

She loosened her grip on him, diving for the glasses.

"God, I can't break these. I'd be blind as a bat without them," she exclaimed. "Twenty bucks each, too."

"I'm sorry," he said, not really meaning it. "I just thought you'd look better without those Bop specs. And you do."

"You're the first fella I've ever been with that's taken my glasses off last. Usually they think it's daring as hell to yank them off, before the first kiss."

"Maybe they think it's part of undressing you, and they haven't the guts to go the rest of the way."

"I wouldn't say that was true in every case."

"Well, let's just say the jokers get a charge out of it," Ken said.

"One night, a guy knocked them off when I wouldn't give. I'm not as easy as this with all the guys, Kenny."

"I know, Baby," he said, grinning up at her. "It's just that I'm such a damn sweet kid."

"You're nice, all right. You're a winner—and you know it." She lay back on his arm. "But, taking everything into consideration, you're a pretty conceited bastard."

The heat made them lazy, drowsy, so that neither felt like rushing into the soul-searing moment that would end this idyllic interlude. Let it build naturally.

Ken had watched this chicken for two or three months, nodding to her every time he passed her typewriter. He knew she liked him because she always lowered her eyes after she had stolen a quick glance. But this afternoon was really a revelation. She had always seemed such a prim little thing. Well, as they said in books, live and learn.

"Sure is hot for Christmas," she said, absently.

"What in hell brought that up?" he asked, sitting up for another drink.

"I was just thinking that if it wasn't for the party this morning, I might never have met you. We might have kept nodding and smiling at each other for the rest of our lives and done nothing about it."

She lay on his shoulder caressing him gently. Keeping the mood bubbling in the background in case they needed it in a hurry.

"What's the matter, Kid?" He took a long sip from the narrow brown mouth of the bottle. "You got it bad for me, huh?"

He waited for the answer, knowing that it would be a lie. It was a game harmless in itself. Which one could make the other believe the biggest lie.

"Bad enough."

"Me too."

"Do you really, Kenny?"

"Do you think I'd be here if I didn't?"

She squirmed around, lying on his stomach, with her softly firm breasts gouging his chest, and her lips, flat, moist and warm against his. He was forced to set his bottle on the nightstand and concentrate on the business at hand.

Her loping breath seared his cheek, and his arms tightened around her spare body. She fitted her knee between his and worked upward.

She knew all the tricks all right, he told himself.

He stretched his arms easily upward, cupping a breast in each gripping hand. Clawing gently, he pulled her down to him. She smothered him again with a loose, burning kiss. As she broke her lips away from his, she sighed gently. Pleading in his ear.

He threw her glasses to the end of the bed again. Her eyes were softly closed and she didn't notice a thing.

The wafting afternoon breeze suddenly became an inferno of pent fury. The constant sound of the automobiles on the highway outside the window turned into a cacophony of raucous sound. The tempo, speeded, rushing faster and faster into a whirling, pulsing maelstrom that would surely suck him out into eternity where he would drift miles beyond the earth's surface, a lost and tiny star, for all time.

He was lost, swallowed up and gone, and it was almost more than he could stand. No matter how he held himself in, tight within the bounds of his own will power, his heartbeat leaped ever faster, as he rose within himself in independent power, a giant within himself, until it seemed that the tissuelike skin of his chest would never contain it. It must surely skip a beat, falter and stop, leaving him gasping his last breath feebly, like a fish out of water; or burst its tiny prison, his rib cage, with a rending crash, and go bounding off, before his eyes, across the shoddy rug, like a grotesque, misshapen, bloody frog, while he lay dying and the girl was slowly throttling the life out of him.

She opened her eyes for a moment, passively waiting his next move.

They both knew that this sequence of events had been building for a long time. It had been on the way since the first or second day she had entered the office as a hireling secretary. She proved her worth and stayed. And as soon as she had seen this lank giant, with the knowing smile, she had promised herself she would have him.

She had been the next youngest of nine; born in a slab-sided, tenant farm cabin in the flats of West Tennessee. She had been a hand-me-down child. Everything she ever had, before she left home, had belonged to someone else first. But not this one. She wouldn't share him with anyone.

She knew that she was no beauty, but in her travels, a few men had found her attractive. Some had discovered in her a piquant bed partner. The questing type that continually searched for new thrills, running the gamut of operations and procedure.

But, the hell with the others that had existed before. Ken was the one. She would bide her time—wait and watch—and some day. . . .

She had handled some of Ken's correspondence, and once they started a small conversation. Shop talk, insurance policies, but a sufficient hook on which to hang a nodding acquaintance. Quietly, she continued to connive.

Sometimes, as he was passing by, a sudden fit of clumsiness would overtake her, and some of her papers fall to the floor.

"Get a basket," he would laugh, eyes crinkling up at her from his stopped position on the floor. He made her heart pant within her breast when he did that trick with his eyes. A sailor she had almost married in Galveston had had the same habit.

But Ken was never friendlier than a casual smile and a flip remark. It worried her.

He was not naïve enough to think she was not interested, but he had no desire to increase their familiarity. His life was complete in itself. His spare evenings he spent in various bars, with three friends he had known before the war. He went along for laughs, happy to do anything the others suggested, concentrating on being a good joe.

Their routine never varied. They would drink one beer in each joint, until they spotted some woman they wanted. Then they went on the make for her. The goal was to sneak a quickie in the back seat of the car. It required tricky timing, because there were four of them, and usually only one car.

Ken had met an occasional girl with an apartment. The guys really sat up when he told them.

Ken knew it was a hell of a way to act, when he had a swell wife like Connie waiting at home, but goddamn it, they had nothing in common any more. She didn't even seem to want him around. She had her crowd and he had his. It wouldn't be too long before they would have to have a showdown, and then the sparks would really fly. If she wanted the whole grimy story laid on the line, he was just the boy that could do it. He used to stay home, once in a while, but when she wasn't out running around, she had a bunch of women over. He didn't believe she even went with any other guy. He didn't have any kick on that score. But she knew so damn many girls. Social work, church work, committees. She probably belonged to every damned committee in Los Angeles County. Like a bunch of locusts when they were at the house. Connie always chased him into the spare bedroom. The one they had always planned for a nursery. And there he would sit, the whole damn night, biting his fingers and smoking one butt after another. And thinking.

The thin blonde with the horn-rimmers. She was on the make, he knew. He could have dated her, taken her to some two-bit joint, and layed her, maybe. He had plenty of free nights, but if Connie ever found out, there'd be hell. Maybe it was a good thing. Get this thing to a head and find out just where they stood.

Ken had thought of taking the blonde out, several times, but always decided against it. Too direct a pipe line from the office to the house.

Of course, Bud, whose desk was next to Ken's thought him a sucker to pass up a sure thing like the blonde filly. Bud was a confirmed bachelor who was willing to endure the benefits of marriage, without assuming any of the responsibilities. A thoroughly integrated man. He probably would have raped the girl right on the office floor, in front of a half hundred other shocked, outraged, and possibly envious stenos, if given half the come-hither that was hung out for Ken.

"Christ, man," he would rant. "Just who do you think you are? One of the twelve sacred vestals? What the hell have you got, that you're trying so hard to protect?"

Ken had tried to protest, but before he could speak, Bud had his meaty palm in the air.

"Okay, okay. So we all know you love your wife," he continued breezily, "what's to stop you from scooping up a little strange stuff on the side? Who's gonna tell mama? Not this one. 'Cause if you're smart, you'll keep it to yourself."

Bud rested a blue jowl on his hand. Contemplated the injured Ken for a moment.

"On the other hand, maybe you are smart. That blond babe latches her eyes onto you like you have been sticking her."

Ken laughed, flicking a cigarette out of his pack. Bud was clearly not the man to share confidences about his extracurricular activities. One hint to him about the lays in the back seat of the car and in the swank apartments, and the entire office would know about it. And Connie shortly after.

"Get off my back, will you, guy?" he stammered. "Don't you ever get tired shoving that needle into me?"

Bud leaned nearer, assuming a quiet, confidential tone.

"No kidding, Ken, I'm serious. I think a little piece on the side is just what you need. You been moping around here for a dog's age. You want to know why? Listen close, 'cause your Uncle Bud's gonna give a short dissertation on the facts of life, running from the birds and bees routine, through the subject of diaphragmatic abrasions.

"No joke, Boy, you want to know why you're all loused up? You're just out of the army, right? You were racing around overseas like a damn snake that's had a bite of Spanish Fly. On the make for anything that would hold still long enough. Then you get shipped home and have to hang around the same dame for the rest of your life. It's enough to drive any guy off his rock. Especially if he figures his wife might feel the same way."

Ken was accustomed to Bud's badgering, though he was unable to understand why Bud assumed that he was so pure and naïve.

"What's the matter, Bud?" Ken asked. "Don't you believe in love?"

"Like I believe in Alice in Wonderland. There's such a thing as love, and it's wonderful. Until you've made the girl. Then, there's just lying and scheming left. Trying to get her the hell out of your hair until you need her again."

Ken raised his eyebrow, admitting the bald truth of Bud's philosophy. At least, it was partly true. But like all broad statements, it didn't take into consideration a wonderful girl like Connie. He gave Bud an abrupt answer, comprising two one-syllable words.

Bud laughed, slapping his hand on the desk with a whack that made three girls look up from their typing.

"I'm not built right. But all the same, Ken, child, you oughta make your pitch for that blonde. She's hot for what you got."

"Maybe I will some day, Buster. Some day." Ken shook another cigarette out of the pack lying on his desk, and turned back to work.

"Don't let the fruit wither on the vine, Pal. That's tender chicken. Ask the man who knows."

Ken had planned the opening moves in the campaign, but, somehow, had never gotten around to carrying them out. The days rolled on relentlessly; a crushing juggernaut of recurring bills and taxes. Ken and Connie having their differences, but forced to fight shoulder to shoulder, in order to stay alive. Struggling vainly to keep one step ahead of the rent and mounting charge accounts. What with one thing and another, Ken had very little time to make an all out advance towards a full time affair. He could not afford a mistress, and he felt that the complications arising from the acquisition of an eight hour, full scale paramour, would be impossible to handle.

It was simple matter of logistics. His defenses would be vulnerable to attack, if he extended his supply line.

In fact, he might never have known the blonde's name, if it hadn't been for the Christmas Brawl at Rocco's.

Most of the other corporations around town, went all out for their employees at the Christmas week end, renting some huge ballroom for the evening, with drinks and entertainment to be deducted, of course, from their corporation tax. But not Los Angeles Mutual. They were adamant that no official party was to be sponsored by the management.

As a result of the tight-lipped attitude of the Board of Directors, it was an unwritten law among the employees that no one ever worked the day before Christmas. The Big Boys on the top floor didn't come out and say, "Merry Christmas—knock off the rest of the day—go home and enjoy the holiday with your folks, friends, loved ones—forget about the job until after the Big Day—have a few Tom and Jerries and a water glass full of Bourbon—" No, the Big Boys never really let the slaves go, but neither did they prevent clerks and stenographers sifting away from whatever job they happened to be doing. Eddying into little groups of murmuring laughter, and at nine sharp, go giggling down to Rocco's. If they had ever made the pretense of going upstairs to the office, in the first place. The outside contact men, office gobbledegook for door-to-door salesmen, made it a point to bring their tally sheets in to the Main on this morning, above all others. No one wanted to miss the fun.

Momentarily, they were free from the pressing thumb of business, and could sit, indulging in the gentle art of oral seduction with some member of the opposite sex that had worked with them for the preceding year. This was the time to find out whether that person preferred the goose or the handshake.

A few Seven Highs under your belt can release an awful lot of inhibitions, and some girl who would look more at home out on the corner, playing first comet in the Salvation Army Band, might be the first one to suggest hitting a motor court for the night.

The back tables in the little joint are packed, and some jokester, smeared with lipstick from top to bottom, always takes it upon himself to unscrew all the light bulbs. Then it's nice and dark. So all the mousy secretaries and the underpaid clerks and salesmen can play kiss and grab the nearest unprotected portion of someone else's lawfully wedded. Indulging in the only indoor sport that isn't taxed. It's a harmless game until it backfires. Then someone usually gets hurt.

If Ken had known that it might happen to him, he might have gone somewhere else. He had been with the firm, slightly more than a year, and the acquaintances he had with L.A.M.L. were people he had met in the bar last Christmas, when he was just out of the service, when everybody was veteran happy and couldn't do enough for them. But now, all that had worn away, just as it does after every war, and the people realize that they have been taken on another military sleigh ride. But, just the same, Ken had been anticipating this impromptu gathering for the last couple of months.

There was nothing he liked better than sitting around with a tall, cold one in his hand, with an eager group hanging on his every sparkling word. One of Ken's most cherished beliefs about himself, one of his special concepts, was that he was as witty as hell, with a few straight shots inside him.

It was ten, before he could get into Rocco's Bar and Grill for the festivities. He might have been an hour earlier, but he was returning from one of the larger department stores with Connie's Christmas present. He had seen it two weeks before, hanging on a window dummy. In spite of the dummy's pecu-liarly pained expression, he could visualize Connie in it. She had to have it.

He had scrimped, borrowed, and finally, two nights ago, he had struck it lucky. He had cleaned the boys for twenty bucks in a two-bit, half-buck poker game. That had put him over the hump, and now he had the seventy-five dollar sharkskin suit in a bundle, under his arm. Connie would be nuts about it.

A raucous bubble of high-pitched, chattering voices, hit him in the face like a wet sponge, as he stepped inside the cool, dim cave.

After the bright glare of the sun outside, the bluish bulbs over the bar might as well have been shut off, for all the good they did Ken. Indistinct forms huddled over the counter, growling and shoving, clinking glasses in spurious good cheer, like some dream from the Inferno. Seeking any excuse to release year-long yokes and restraints.

Ken passed down the narrow passage, between the press of people and the wall, nodding and receiving his share of slaps on the back. Seeking the back room. He had promised Bud he would meet him there. That's where the action would be, if there was any this early in the morning.

Seeing a vacant spot at the bar, he moved in, signaling the barkeep.

"Hey, Rocco," Ken shouted, holding the precious sharkskin bundle over his head. "Stick this under the bar, huh? Pick it up later. And a Seven High. Okay?"

The bartender spoke around a cold, green cigar.

"Bud was here. Said to tell you he's inna back. Says he's got a surprise for you."

"Yeah, I'll bet."

Feeling the cold dew on the outside of his glass, Ken pushed away from the bar. As he entered the smoky room, he saw Bud tilted back in his chair, balancing precariously on two legs, and surveying the five people at his table with the cold, calculating expression of a fish.

"Probably trying to figure which of the three babes will be the easiest go," Ken told himself. "Even if he has to belt one of the other guys on the skull. And, if I know Bud, he's feeding plenty of shots to everyone concerned, to make it simpler."

In the office, Bud was known as "The Operator." He was always working on a big deal, or needed two bucks for a sure thing at the track. He was always looking for the smooth way out, but nothing ever seemed to pan out. He had made certain enemies with his condescending manner. They said that if anybody happened to throw a rock at the boss's tail, it. would hit Bud right in the back of the neck.

But despite all his efforts at self-elevation, Bud still had the desk next to Ken's. Ken bore him no ill will, the fact being, that he admired Bud's sardonic outlook, trying to emulate it in his own fashion. And Bud, sensing this left-handed form of idolatry, accepted Ken as one of his own. Of course the older man's method of acceptance was hard to endure, at times, but Ken rolled with the mental punches and came back swinging.

Bud's chair hit the floor as he saw Ken enter the room. He waved wildly, nearly toppling to the floor. Ken saw the so-called surprise immediately. It was the blonde with the enormous glasses. She was clutching a shot glass, half full, and she turned to him and smiled, as he pulled up a chair beside her.

What the hell. Might as well go all the way, if that was what was expected of him.

"Knew you'd be along soon," Bud chortled. "That's what I told Beverly Jean. Didn't I, Beverly, Honey Chile?"

So that was her name.

"Sure, Buddy boy." Her accent was a mixture of magnolia blossoms and coffee cream. "You told me to hang around, 'cause Blondie here would show up in a minute."

"Well, ole Bud don't tell no lies, do he," Bud mimicked.

Beverly Jean smiled, dipping her pert nose demurely into her shot glass.

"Jeez, I'm forgettin' all my bringin' up," Bud waved his hand lazily between the two. "Beverly Jean Hartley, this is Kenny Lawrence, and vice versa. God, Kenny, where you been? I thought you weren't going to show."

"I had some Christmas shopping." He smiled at the blonde, acknowledging the introduction, feeling that this was not the time to say who the shopping had been for.

He turned to case the table.

There were two other typewriter girls and a couple of fellows Ken hadn't seen before. He nodded around, mumbling the usual cliches, as he was introduced. The men were older than himself, auditors from the third floor. His desk was on Two, and he had no contact with them. They were quite drunk, and quite identical. Dime cigar smouldering in the corner of the mouth, tilting glasses, each time another traveling-salesman-and-the-farmer's-daughter stinker went the rounds. They pawed at the table, the girls, the drinks, each other, and the girls again. Evidently Bud was pitching some angle, working these knuckleheads for something, because his boredom was showing through. Ken knew that Bud had these birds classified as sure losers.

"It's good to see you, Ken boy," Bud said, laying the opaque charm thickly around him. "Where you been keeping yourself? Sorry, I just asked that two minutes back. With all this damn noise in here, you can't hear yourself think."

"Christmas comes but once a year," Ken said, conscious that the bromide fell flat.

He couldn't let himself down into the crowd. He was on a different plateau, above, or below, their level. It didn't matter which, but he couldn't get in among them and lose himself in their gaiety. To giggle at senseless meanings, contrived associations. They had a fine start on him, and he wanted to catch up with this easy world that, for now, was bounded by the walls of this cramped and dingy back room. Where there are no clocks, and the time is always right now.

Beverly spoke as though she had been reading his mind.

"Let me spike that Seven Up for you, Boy. You're way behind."

She placed a purse on her lap that looked more like a brief case, rummaged around in it for a moment, pulling forth, finally, a pint of bourbon. She deftly flipped off the cap, evidencing long practice, and let a generous slug bubble into Ken's glass.

"This stuff isn't quite as good as ham and eggs, but Baby had it for breakfast this morning," she said. "And speaking of morning, what's it like upstairs?"

"Quiet," Ken said, sipping from his glass.

"Well, it's like you said. Christmas comes but once a year. Thank God."

Ken knew that she was almost out of sight, down the road to complete stupidity. She was getting louder, and as he watched, she lit another cigarette, although she had one burning in the ash tray. He had a feeling that today might be the day.

He sized her up from a utility standpoint. Her large, swooping breasts took his breath away, amazing him. She appeared lithe and rapid. She might prove to be quite a handful in bed.

"Here's hoping," he murmured. He raised his glass alone and drank to his own success.

The blonde had another toast.

"Here's to the Christ Child," she said. "It's a shame he had to die for us drunks, but that's life."

Ken nodded absently, catching part of the joke Bud was telling the auditors, intent on downing the bourbon bombshell that the blonde had fixed him. It gagged him, and his throat constricted. There is such a thing as getting too much whiskey in a drink. Especially the first one of the morning.

"It's funny that you and I have been speaking for almost three months, and I just found out your name. Ken Lawrence," Beverly said, rolling the name back and forth on her tongue, savoring the sound of it.

"What's so funny about it?" he laughed. "My name can't do you any good. It's not on the bottom of your pay check."

"You don't want to say that, Boy. You can't tell when your name might come in real handy. Someone to go my bail, or something."

"A sweet kid like you. You've never seen the inside of a jail."

"Have you?"

"Hell, no. And I'm happy about it, don't you think I'm not."

Ken felt much better about the whole thing. Things were working out. The brick burn of the bourbon had flattened out to the tips of his tiniest capillaries and his muscles were beginning to relax. The world was slowly assuming a rosy glow.

"How's your drinkin' liquor holdin' out?" Beverly asked.

Ken tilted his glass, draining the last drop of nectar.

"Hold it. I gotta get another set-up."

"Take your time goin'. But hurry back." She smiled up at him as he rose to his feet.

Ken caught Bud's eye, motioning his head in the direction of the bar. Without interrupting his story, Bud handed his glass up for a refill. Letting the punch line go in a snigger of laughter.

" ... well, let's take these damn things off then."

The auditors doubled up, trying to burn each other with the ridiculous cigars they held in their mouths. The women appeared properly shocked.

As he threaded his way through an even thicker press of humanity, toward the bar, Ken decided that the two girls were trying to let down as desperately as he was. Probably didn't know how, without losing precious dignity.

How little you really know about the people you spend the majority of your waking hours with, Ken thought. You work within touching distance of them for eight hours a day, and all their carefully constructed shells are raised as a barrier between you. They are prim, sedate, faceless. When you catch them with their guard down, in a place like this, they turn out to be just anybody. Wild animals, with all the instincts of the jungle out in the open, where you can see them and read them for what they are. Rampaging loose, with the thin veneer of civilization, dropping away like a decaying ash.

Who'd have thought the little blonde with the studious air, smiling her demure, impersonal smile, worn like a badge of impartiality, could turn into a saucy babe that would pack a pint in her purse. Live and learn.

He could be free and easy too. That was the way to handle a piece like that. He would have to relax and get into the groove.

He returned to the table with the shots and the frosted, tinkling glasses, and sat down with a sigh of relief.

"What's that character, Bud, got on his mind?" Beverly whispered. "He's pouring whiskey into the Auditing Department."

"Working some angle, Bev. But I'm darned if I can figure it," Ken answered.

She flared, whirling on him.

"Don't ever call me that. Beverly Jean, or just Beverly. Or even better, Darling."

"Why no nickname?"

"My Daddy used to call me that back home. He was a son-of-a-bitch."

Ken smiled, pouring some bourbon into her glass from the bottle on the floor.

"To coin a cliche."

Her eyes had started to glass up, as she laid her hand on his shoulder.

"You can laugh if you want, Blondie. But it isn't so damn funny when you know the facts."

Ken took another swallow. The stuff was beginning to get to him. He wanted to be at Beverly's level. Then he could give her the false sympathy she needed. That would put her on his side for sure.

He would just have to do the best he could.

"What's the trouble, Hon? You got a grudge?" He found himself stroking her hair.

"Against my Daddy? Hell, yes. He gave me so much bad time, messin' 'round, I finally had to leave home, when I was fifteen. He wouldn't ever leave me alone. Always fingerin' and foolin' around. I had three sisters and my Ma, and I was the only one he ever bothered. There was so many of us and I was the only one that had my own room, just so's he could sneak up at night, without anyone knowin'. Every time I get on a little jag, I get riled at him all over again."

Ken felt a mixture of amusement and contempt. He was trying to believe her story.

"What did you do after you left home? Fifteen's a pretty tender age."

"I lived with an aunt. Worked in a mill in Nashville."

"You're pretty smart to come out of a mill in Nashville."

"I put myself through business school at night."

"I don't want to be nosy. You don't have to answer me, you know."

"Go ahead. I don't mind."

She gazed into his eyes, clear and steady for the moment. Without shifting her gaze, she placed his glass in his hand, clinking it with her own.

"To us. May this be a beautiful friendship." She smiled slowly.

"Just one more question. Okay?"

"I said, go ahead, didn't I?"

Ken was convinced of several things now. That her story was the truth. But the major thing was that she would be his completely, within the next few hours. That was what stayed up in front of his mind.

"How come you're 'way out here on the coast?" he asked. "How did you come to leave Nashville?"

"I thought we'd come to that, Kenny," she said, her eyes on the table, glass turning nervously in her hand. "I don't know how to start telling you. It's funny, but I can let up with you; probably because you have an understanding look. I feel that I can tell you anything and you'll know the reason behind why I've done some of the things I've done. You won't condemn me for some of the cheap tricks I've pulled, and you'll know why I had to do them at the time. Are you flattered at these true confessions? I haven't told many people about the mean, rotten life I've led. And for God's sake, don't spread it around."

"Why the hell should I?" he answered, assuming a confidential attitude, with his head close to hers. "It's really none of my business, is it? It'll stop here."

They were interrupted by the auditors struggling to their collective feet. Sensing Bud's play, they had decided to take their women and leave.

"C'mon, girls. We're goin'."

Bud sat staring quietly into his glass for a few minutes. A wide smile crossed his swarthy face.

"Well, let's not sink the ship, because those rats jumped off," he laughed. "What are you guys drinking?"

"Even me," Ken thought. "You'd give me the shaft too, if you thought I'd stand still for it. But not this time."

"We're not drinking in here any more, Bud. We're going out west aways and see what they have to offer. Aren't we, Darling." Ken emphasized the last sentence carefully, loading it with unmistakable meaning.

Beverly snagged the cue quickly.

"That's what the man said. We're just gettin' ready to leave, Mr. Bud."

"Okay," Bud said, taking a healthy swallow. "No hard feelings, huh?"

"No revenge." Ken playfully punched his arm. "It was almost a good try."

Beverly stowed her pint in her purse, and she and Ken pushed out into the blistering heat. The sun blasted them, and even the sidewalk seemed to shimmer in the heat.

A couple of blocks later, they turned into a parking lot filled with glittering chrome and steel. Ken's car stood near the drive. An old one, with a new appearance. He shoveled seventy-five into the attendant's palm, and the little Ford pointed west.

"Do you really think Bud was on the make for both those girls?" Beverly fumbled in her bag for a cigarette.

"I know it. That sucker doesn't maneuver that way for kicks."

"But what would he do with two women? Most men can't handle one with any starling success." She sipped at the neck of the bottle she produced from her purse.

"Probably had a friend waiting with an apartment."

"He's certainly got a lot of nerve. You got to say that for him."

"That's only half the story. When he saw his play with the Auditing Department fold, he tried to open up a beachhead on you."

Ken glanced over at her to check her reaction.

High, choking laughter.

"That greasy slob. I wouldn't give him a break any place, but across his spine."

The bonded that Ken had consumed was singing a happy song in his head. He was humming to himself as he herded his little car along the gulfstream of vehicles, looking like an avalanche of mechanized ants, winding west through MacArthur Park.

She gave another snort of laughter, and he looked across at her again.

"What's your story?" he asked.

"It's just that damn Bud. It seems I run into a jerk like that, no matter where I go."

"Oh, he's not such a bad kid when you get to know him."

"I know him all right. And there's no market for his kind of kids."

For Christ sake, fella, what're you doing, Ken asked himself. Let it drop, you'll be getting her sore. Are you out of your head completely? She'll be calling a taxi in a minute.

And the other side of him whispered back. Why not risk it a little further. What if you do lose out. All you've really lost, is some little chippie you'll never remember twenty years from now anyway. After all, Bud's done right by you in his own way. Just try it a little more and see where it goes.

Ken patted her knee.

"I know Bud tried to knife me in the back just now," he said, "but that's just his way. You've got to expect that with Bud. It's always him against the world."

"You're not sticking up for him, I hope."

"Why not? I like the guy. He's got a swell personality."

"He's got a personality like a lead pipe. He's one of these guys that always have to be big shots. No matter how low they are, what street they're sweeping, what junk pile they're sifting, looking for a bite to eat, they always imagine they're right up there on top. No, he's no good, Ken. He'll foul you up every time. Stick with me, Boy. I'm good for you."

"That's nice, Hon." Ken decided this was the time to forget the whole thing. "I'm good for you too."

The world outside the coupe was nothing but wonderful. Everywhere Ken looked, he saw harried shoppers bustling in and out of the swank shops along Wilshire's Miracle Mile, buying armloads of toys, neckties, Argyles and perfume. It was almost worth the struggle to be alive today.

Passing a store window, crammed with mannequins, he remembered Connie's suit, with a shock.

Under the bar at Rocco's! Christ!

He fought back an impulse to make a U turn in the middle of the block.

Should he turn around, go all the way back for the suit, he asked himself. Wouldn't it be totally destroying to the mood he had carefully built in Beverly? It wouldn't sound so hot to her, after she had more or less offered herself to him, to hear him say: "Sorry, honey, but I have to go back and pick up my wife's Christmas present."

Besides, the suit would be okay, right where it was. He could drop by for it, after he had seen Beverly home, he rationalized.

Another shattering thought hit him with such force that he ran a red light. This was a problem of blinding importance, and stemmed naturally from the convolutions of the Christmas suit.

The purchase of that little item had left him with one single five-dollar bill rattling around in his pocket. And he had spent two in Rocco's bar. He had been so engrossed in whisking Beverly out of Bud's grasp, that he had forgotten that he couldn't finance his play.

How was he going to break it to her?

Might as well get the show on the road.

"Where do we go from here?" he opened up.

"Anywhere you say, Darling. I'm easy to please."

He drove in silence, glancing at her occasionally, checking the fine points of her figure. Her wild thighs, as their contours appeared through the fold of her light dress. Her slim, capable hips. Speculating on her competency.

He would have to make out somehow. He had to have her. The liquor was fast coming to a head.

Even the ridiculous glasses seemed attractive now.

"This Christmas season is sure rough," he said, starting off in a new direction.

"I know what you mean."

"I had to buy presents for everybody in Los Angeles County, this year."

"And because of same, you're a little short. Is that what you're trying to tell me? And you want to let me off easy, because you're broke."

His eyes rigidly on the road, Ken nodded silently.

Beverly hesitated before answering. She lit a cigarette, pressing it between Ken's lips with caressing fingers. She took a long swallow from the bottle.

"Look," she said finally, "I've got something to tell you, and if you ever let it out, I'll kill you."

"Don't worry. What is it?"

"I may not look it, but I've been around, quite a lot in my young life. Always running away, afraid to face tomorrow. I started to tell you back there," she gestured clumsily, her voice beginning to blur at the edges, "about my life. I've never been a saint. What girl can afford to be these days? But I haven't been a chippy either. I got married, had a good one, one with a barrel of dough. But he was like a damn rabbit. I wasn't the only one he had on the line."

"So?" Ken asked.

"So, I got rid of him, with a decree in my favor. With alimony. And it just so happens, that I have a wad of it with me now. If you haven't too much pride to go out, on me, we can make a night of it."

"We'll call it a loan. I'll pay you back as soon as I get straightened out."

"I used to know a guy in Texas, once, who always borrowed money from me. It was always 'Slip me five until the weather breaks,' or, 'Put me on the books for ten, until my brother straightens out. He's a hunchback.' "

"Did you give it to him?"

"Yes, and he never paid me back. He went down in the Coral Sea, owing me three hundred dollars."

"Was he the one?" Ken asked, softly.

"He was the only one, ever, for me. I went up to see his folks after the war. It was just like visiting my own people again. They didn't have nothin', just like my folks. Tenant farmers, with no brains, no land, and hardly any crop. It made me want to sit down and bawl."

Ken glanced at her in pity. Having a lover die on you could ruin any woman. It wouldn't do to change the subject too soon. Beverly was getting a certain amount of perverse enjoyment from parading her grief. Let it alone for a minute. It would only make her mad. This was her personal cross that she bore, just as he carried his shattered marriage on his conscience.

He pulled the car into a side street. It might be better just to sit quiet and talk.

"Is this what made you so…" He gestured with his hand, vaguely. "So—dissatisfied with life. So—don't give a damn?"

"That, and a few other things. It's too Goddamn morbid." She reached for the bottle. "Give me another shot, before I blow my cork."

"No kidding, though," Ken said, sensing that hidden in their words might be an aspect of his own problem. That by talking, he might come nearer his own solution. "Don't you believe that there is a perfect form of love that comes rarely? When two people are so close, mentally and physically, that intuitively, they can feel when something is wrong with one another?"

"That's the way it was with us," she said, staring intently at the burning cigarette she held in her lap. "But it works the other way, too. When you're too long away from the one you love, something seems to slip out of gear. The precious thing vanishes, and you can never find it again. The moment you look that love straight in the face, the second you begin to doubt it, it is gone, and no matter how hard you try to reconstruct it, it'll never be the same. There's such a fine line between a true love and a complete hate. I wonder if I'd have married him, if he had come back."

"I think you've got it," Ken shouted. "Your interests are entirely different. You don't see things from the same outlook as before. Your sense of values will never be the same again. And the parted lovers will never dovetail in their desires again."

Ken's vehemence made Beverly's eyebrows slowly raise.

"Do you think this little escapade is going to solve things for you?" she asked.

"What do you mean?"

"Don't get coy. You know what I mean. I'm just an excuse for you. Because you've no doubt got a lovely wife, and a couple of children at home. And also, because when you and she are momentarily out of time, you use interludes like this, and others like it, for a pressure valve. To bolster your own ego. It's a small, selfish way to do it. At the expense of a defenseless woman. But you men are all alike."

Ken didn't like this twist of the situation at all.

"You're crazy. How did you figure all that nonsense out?"

"Now the little boy is whistling in the dark, isn't he?"

"Are you still serious about going? Or would you rather forget about going out with a married man?"

"Sure I am. I'm starved for a good time."

He looped his arm around her shoulder, bringing her close to him. Her lips were warm, as they kissed.

"You didn't have to do that to shut me up," she said. "I don't give a damn about your private life. I'm small and selfish myself. I want you as much as you want me, so why should I kid myself?"

"I didn't kiss you, because I wanted to drop the subject," he lied. "I did it, because I wanted to see how you kiss."

"Will I do?" she laughed.

"You bet. Bring your lunch and punch in at eight."

He kissed her again, flipping the key in the switch, tromping the engine into life.

In another deep, cool bar, while the bartender was mixing them one, Beverly gently laid her hand in his. As he opened it, he felt a crumpled wad of paper her hand had held, passed to him. For a moment, he thought it was a note, but upon closer scrutiny, in the glowing darkness, it proved to be a twenty-dollar bill. He slid it across the bar, as their drinks were set before them.

The change paid for several rounds.

The bourbon acted quickly on their empty stomachs, and after an hour of desultory conversation, Beverly said, in a conspiratorial tone, "You can't kid me, Blondie. You're married and I know it, and I don't give a damn."

Ken hedged. He was feeling somewhat more than a glow, but out of a curious respect for Connie, he hesitated to tell a flat lie about their marriage. The trouble was that he never could decide whether or not he loved her. He certainly didn't love anyone else; he reflected, he would probably never again know that sweet, driving passion the two of them had shared in the beginning.

"Where did you dream that up?" He stalled.

She inhaled sharply, and her breasts rose tightly against the material of her dress, as the smoke filled her lungs. She watched the wispy white fog drift easily from her mouth, until she was empty of it, before she answered.

"Two things. First, it's human nature for a fellow to make a big splash the first time he takes a girl out, even if it's just honky-tonkin'. What makes the greatest impression? Knowing people. Being able to walk into a bar and knowing the bartender. So what do you do? You hustle me into a joint you've never been in before. Second…"

"Brilliance, sheer brilliance."

"Nonsense. It was easy."

"And the second reason, now that you're being so smug?"

"Okay. Second, because that's the way it's always been. Everything I've always wanted has already been taken by someone else. An hour late and a dollar short. That's the story of my life."

"For Lord's sake, knock it off. Why the blues? Tomorrow's Christmas, remember?"

"I remember," she said, deep in her throat.

"Then why the sobs?"

"I keep thinking of those phony angels. Even in those days, they were shills for the house. Peddling their rotten slogans."

"Who're you kidding?"

They sipped their drinks, reflectively, neither intruding on the other's silence. Their glasses empty, Beverly placed two cigarettes in her mouth, lighting them both. She gave one to Ken, with a lingering touch of her hand.

Ken glanced at the tiny alarm clock, nestled close to the black, gleaming cash register, amid a vast array of varied bottles, on the other side of the bar. One o'clock. Time to get this show on the road.

"You and I make a good team," he began.

"Yeah, we're making out fine. I like your style, Boy. Stick with me, and I'll have your name in lights, six feet high."

His hand tightened on her thigh, and he felt her muscles contract under his fingers. It made his blood boil with desire. He thought of what had been promised him and leaned across and gently bit the lobe of her ear. Her head turned toward him, and she looked deep into his eyes. Without saying a word, she nodded her head.

"Thanks just the same," he said, patting her thigh again, this time, a shade farther up, "but if the price for fame is my pure and spotless name, I must say no—and again, no."

Beverly laughed at him out of her cat's eyes, tilting her head to clear the smoke from her glasses. She waited eagerly for more sales talk.

"No jive, Babe, I honestly don't think two people can really be close to each other, until they've made good, solid love, together. Everything else is just froth, sham and make-believe."

"Do tell now."

"Everybody that spends time necking in the dark," he continued, "or kissing under the mistletoe, for that matter, is only shopping for one thing. And if they go away without it, they wind up with nothing but frustration.

"Don't you think I'm right? Subconsciously, they're all after the same thing, only most of the silly little dodos that spend their time wrapped up in each other's arms up lover's lane, or some other dark corner, either haven't got the brains or the courage to rent a hotel room or a motor court, and spend the night together in a nice, honest bed. And with no strings attached, and no holds barred."

"I agree," Beverly said, sipping. She was quite drunk, warm as a kitten under a stove. "I've been out with fellows that had me practically stripped, in the back seat of their car, but because that seemed to be the outer limit of their experience, they never carried the ball past the ten yard line. I was so damn mad, I could have choked. Talk about frustration."

"Do you realize," Ken went on with mock authority, "that more than ninety percent of the assaults in this country, stem directly from the fact that eighty percent of the population of these United States is sexually frustrated?"

"I'd hate to feel that I was to blame for any of that."

"You might just be party of the first part in a rape case, if we don't find a motor court soon."

"You close in fast, once your mind is made up, don't you?" she said, mockingly.

"Sure, why not? Once you've found the bargain you want, why shop around for anything else?"

"Remember the old Hindu saying? 'Married men have no time to play around. They have to hit and run.' "

"Perhaps," he said, "but they also guarantee good service. Based on years of satisfactory performance."

"You sound like a damn used car salesman, or a pimp for a stallion."

"I'm my own agent. Have I got any takers?"

"Can't let a bargain like this slip by." She swayed toward him, her soft, cool lips touching his, until she felt him press eagerly forward. Then she pulled away quickly. "You know a good place we can go, honey? This girl wants a bed or nothing. No back seats. I want to relax and enjoy you. This one's been a long time coming."

"I have a friend. But it's quite a ways east of here."

"I've got time. Let's find your friend. And stop for another jug, the pint's almost vanished."

In unison, they clinked glasses and drank, banging them back to the counter when empty. Slowly, they slid off the high stools and sauntered into the open sunlight, arm in arm.

The sun was a glaring searchlight, and the heat pinpointed them, specks on the floor of a concrete canyon. For the first few moments, after emerging from the alcoholic cave, they were totally blinded by the contrast.

"Whew!" Ken exclaimed. "I'm loaded."

"Likewise. We've really been packin' it away."

"You can play that again. There's not much of your twenty left."

"Don't fret about it, lover. There's more where that came from."

Ken started forward, but fell back against the wall. Christ, what an afternoon.

"This heat is getting me," he said. "I'm so looped, I doubt if I can drive. Can you take over, Co-pilot? How's it with you?"

"Worse. We'd be a cinch bet for the Lincoln Heights tank. How about a cab?"

"It's a hell of a ways. It'd cost a fortune."

"I'm paying the bill and I'm not squawking. Why should you?"

Ken dug around in his pocket, until he had located a nickel, and they went back into the bar. The two of them crowded cozily into the tiny booth, Beverly fitting her generous breasts tightly against his chest, and he could feel the delightful pressure of her muscled thighs and the soft yield of her stomach against him, and it was impossible to concentrate on anything as she buried her mouth in his neck and nibbled at him with her lips. It made a tingle run the length of him. It made him want to scrunch lower so he could feel the center of her warmth. His free hand, groping, found her breast and cupped it gently, but disappointedly, he found there was not much to be gotten through two or three layers of clothing; the last being a ribbed uplift brassiere.

That was the trouble with women, Ken thought, as he dialed a number he found scrawled on the wall. So goddamn many restraining garments. Corsets, garter belts, panties, uplifts. It was like watching them unscrew their cork leg, flip out a glass eye, and drop a set of teeth in a glass of water, to watch them undress. Not to mention falsies.

How did that old joke go? Oh yeah.

"Throw it over here, honey, you know what I want."

He didn't think Beverly wore any synthetic chest stretchers. When she strutted around the office, she jiggled too convincingly to have anything but that of her own manufacture.

He didn't condemn a girl for accentuating her best points. Got to toot your own horn. But Connie. She never had any use for sham. Having been generously endowed with mammalia, she always said that falsies should be outlawed. Took away the edge that a well built girl had, she told him once. And the way they make them these days, she said, who could tell the difference, until the crucial moment?

The old saying: "What God has forgotten—We fill with Cotton."

Ken massaged Beverly's breast gently. Soft, yet firm. Warm. The nipple like a tiny, hard marble.

He gave his message to the cab company and hung up. Stooping to kiss her in the dim glow of the overhead light. She bored her mouth into his, fierce, with the threat of vicious teeth, hard behind her eager lips.

They broke for air, and she smiled at him with a softness in her eyes.

Ken opened the door, and they squeezed out. They stood in the cool dark, lighting cigarettes, silently savoring the tingling warmth that stole over them as they thought of the moments to come. A horn sounded outside, and they left.

Ken gave the driver an address on East Garvey.

The hackie's eyebrows raised.

"That's a long haul."

"We've got the fare."

"Okay, Pal. It's your ride. But it's going to cost."

As soon as the cab pulled away from the curb, Ken and Beverly fell into a clinch, tight as though they were starved for each other and hadn't been together for years. Their lips met and clove together, time and timeless time again, and their restless hands clutched and clawed and did wondrous things, arousing passion that had been long stifled. Ken's tapering fingers performed miracles that he hadn't seen in Connie for months, just grazing them gently along Beverly's upper thigh, under the sheer material of her step-ins, causing her to crouch a degree lower, seeking him blindly. Almost as soon as their lips touched, they were probing each other with their mouths, working silently in a tight embrace, sending an almost electric charge through their bodies.

The cab stopped with a sudden jolt that nearly set them on the floor. They were tightly wrapped in each other's arms, and it took a split second for them to snap apart.

"What the hell ... ?" Ken shouted.

The cab driver turned in his seat, frowning.

"I don't care what you do after you leave me, but you're not going to make a bedroom out of my taxi. There's a place for everything, and my cab's a place of business."

"Why do you give a damn? You're getting paid, aren't you?"

"Fella, it's a question of ethics. I don't allow no messin' in the back of my hack, and no motor court owner hauls his customers around in his car. A kind of a laisser-faire."

Beverly had covered her mouth with the back of her hand, until she could hold it no longer. She leaned back against the seat and laughed.

"Christ, this is rich. A lecture on morals from a cab driver."

"Not morals, girlie," the driver explained meticulously, "Ethics. Ethics you might understand."

"Meaning?"

"Meaning just what you might interpret yourself."

Cagey old devil, Ken thought. Telling us we're a couple of tramps, horsing around in broad daylight, in the only way he can get away with it. And the day before Christmas. He's right, but the hell with him. Bev's too potent to call this thing off now.

"These philosophers all give me a pain," Beverly said. "They've been so damn busy staying up nights, solving all the world's problems, they've never taken any time to let loose and live a little. And they don't want anyone else to have any fun, either. Complete with reasons as to why you shouldn't."

"Leave the old crackpot alone," Ken placated. "After we get where we're going, he can peddle his message to someone else."

Though he sounded impervious, the cabbie's unmistakable inferences had struck home. Ken's mind flew back to the comforting thought of Connie, like a homing bird. The things she might be doing this afternoon, like beating the heat in shorts and bra. How she looked, early in the morning, watching him drink his coffee, softly curling jet hair, loose from restraining pins, caressing her shoulders with its cascading length, contrasting with her scarlet housecoat. And Connie's presence in his mind, instilled a certain passivity in him that was never completely dispelled the rest of the afternoon.

They had stopped for another supply of bourbon, as they passed through Gabriel, in spite of a silent, disapproving pout from their driver. And had paid him off with something not too far removed from happiness and relief, when they reached their destination.

"Mark what I say," he had said, with his hand outstretched. "You two won't go far. They'll get to you. They'll hit you where you live."

"Hockey," Beverly retorted, tongue waggling at him.

Ken took her arm, piloting her uncertainly up the graveled walk toward a row of shabby, sun-blistered cabins.

"Forget him," Ken said. "The old bastard gives me a pain I can't scratch in public."

"What a case," Beverly laughed.

"There's one in every crowd."

The blonde nodded in the direction of the cabin they were approaching, adorned with the inevitable rain streaked, dirty sign, reading, "Manager."

"Do you think we can get in this place without being tossed out on our fannies? I forgot to bring my wedding ring. It usually comes in handy on a deal like this."

"Forget it. I tell you, I know the guy. Went to school with him. His Dad used to own it, and he had a heart attack and left it to Joe. It used to be a hell of a lot nicer than it is now. Joe's been busy drinking up the little money his old man left him, and he just hasn't had time to take care of the place. It's really gone to hell in a hurry."

"You've been here before then?"

"Do you care?"

"Not a damn. I like my men with experience. As long as I'm picking up the tab, I want to be sure I'm getting the best. I've been waiting a long time."

They stepped inside the office, and it looked just as bad as the outside. Ash trays loaded with week-old butts, half smoked cigarettes lying where they had been mashed into the floor with a careless heel, days ago; a beer can lying on its side under a straight backed chair. A bottle of something, with an inch left in the bottom, stood beside an ancient cash register. An odor of food standing long in the can pinched the nostrils and hung like a presence in the humid air.

A lank man, unshaven, with eyes showing tiny red veins, like the silk hairs in a dollar bill, stood up as they entered.

"Hiya, Ken," he pumped Ken's hand. "Where ya been keepin' yourself? You been out of circulation?"

"I was down a couple of weeks ago. You were gone. Had a sign on the door, 'Gone Fishing.' "

"Oh yeah, I remember now. I was shacked up with a chippie over at the Villa in Catalina. She and her girl friend are a couple of school teachers out here on a vacation from Sioux Falls. She said when they're on the job, they can't drink, smoke, and if they're caught with a man, the ramrods of the town would tar 'n feather 'em. So they come out here to let their hair down. And there I was every night—from one.... "

He broke off, as Beverly stepped from behind Ken.

"Pardon me, lady, I just.... " Joe stammered.

"I know. That's all right. I was young once myself." She smiled.

"This your wife?" Joe smiled back, glancing slyly at Ken.

"Yeah," Ken growled.

"For today. Right now," Beverly added.

"It's like that, huh?" A trace of a smile tugged at the corners of Joe's mouth. "Isn't there a state law or a county ordinance against shacking indiscriminately."

"We aren't doing this indiscriminately, Joe," Beverly said. "It's premeditated. We picked each other out."

"It don't matter. I can't remember the fool law anyway. So I'll have to let you have a room. There's nobody else staying here, so you can just take your pick. After you've signed the register, according to the law that I do know."

They signed.

Herman Diddler and Wife, Galveston.

Beverly dredged around in her handbag, bringing the new pint to light.

"Have a shot, Mr. Joe?"

Without a word, Joe reached eagerly for the bottle. He let the bourbon trickle slowly down his throat, as though it were cool, spring water. Ken went behind the counter, lifting a key from the board. He laid a bill on the table and snagged the bottle from Joe's hand. They started toward the door.

"Don't let your engine overheat," Joe shouted after them. "You gotta watch for vapour lock in this kind of weather."

"I don't want you to come sneakin' around out back, peeking through the blind," Ken said, pointedly.

"How you talk," Joe was wounded. "Treat this boy right, Woman, he's a good one."

"You tell him to do right by me," Beverly retorted. "I'm pretty nice myself."

And now, as they pounded into the final contortions, straining, fighting the last and greatest culminating act of the entire afternoon, the meaning of the whole day, Ken was attacked by qualms of conscience. He hated himself for being so weak and undecided. The whole thing had been perfect. Beverly had been all that he had desired and more. Tender and soothing, rough, fiercely demanding, dissolving him into her gently undulating curves, like rain into the parched earth. But, after this last final urge, what?

4:00 P.M.

THE SPUN GLOSS of her black hair lay in a fine web over the pillow, and she dozed lightly. Her shoulders were bare, well formed with enough flesh to conceal the hollows at the collarbone. The clear, cool skin of her body, deepening into the curved, promising crevice of her breasts, looked darker than it actually was, by contrast against the white percale drawn over her, just enough to conceal the apex, the rising and falling summit, of generous, ivory breasts.

The girl lay flat, legs slightly extended in sleep, completely relaxed. Her figure was concealed from view, but even as the actual detail of it was hidden, the law of gravity conspired with the light sheet, presenting the form and delightful hollows and convolutions of it to the eye.

She was long, slim and straight. Length of trunk and the thin, tapering legs, told of a wiry competence in performing wifely duties. If she so desired, she could hold any man spellbound with her complete beauty of form. Her narrow waist and slim hips would lend enchantment, whether encased in a pair of slacks or a frilly party dress. And make a man's heart catch in his throat if seen without either.

The cheekbones made tiny shelves under her eyes, giving her an almost Oriental look. Her nose was straight and narrow at the nostrils.

She slept, beauty in repose, two tiny teeth caught over her full lower lip, until the telephone shrilled, blasting her out of bed.

Her eyes were tightly closed as she fumbled with the clothes heaped at the foot of the bed. She wore only tiny panties, until she grappled forth a scarlet housecoat. Painfully, she funneled into it and groped her way to the door.

The living room of the tiny house was stifling. She opened her eyes wearily, sitting on the couch, catching the 'phone in her left hand.

"Yes?" she said as though she hoped the party on the other end might happily drop dead.

"Hello, Gladys. I thought it might be you. ... What are the other girls planning? .... Well, you know Ken. His company has some sort of Christmas celebration every year. He'll probably come home stupid again, like he did last year."

A long pause as she listened.

"You know, darling, it's just like I always said. If that's the kind of life he wants to lead, I'm certainly not going to be the one to stop him. He just isn't the same as when we were married. Something's slipped someplace. ... It could be my fault too. . Oh, I don't imagine it's anything to worry about. ... It'll all work out somehow. ... Don't worry about it. ... I was in bed. ... Yes, you woke me up. ... That's all right I had to get up anyway."

She reached across to a small, glass topped coffee table, taking a cigarette out of a ceramic box. Ornate, with china pansies on the lid. She lit the cigarette, puffing lightly. Listening.

"I wouldn't mind going to a show tonight. Ken? He won't care. He'll probably be wobbly and want to find the bed as soon as he can. Or go bowling with Sammy or somebody. ... Certainly I trust him when he goes out with Sammy. Why shouldn't I? He trusts me when I go out with you. ... But that only happened once. And he was so cute. ... When is the next club meeting? .... All right. 'Bye now."

After she replaced the receiver, she went into the scarlet and yellow kitchen, with the ruffled curtains faintly stirring at the windows, and turned the flame under the aluminum percolator. She stretched, luxuriously, placing her hands at the back of her neck, under the long strands of black hair, tensing every fibrous muscle, to the tops of her toes. The swelling mounts of her breasts, strained against her thin garment, the aureoles visible in bas-relief. She was oblivious of the picture she made.

Gazing out of the window that faced the street, she watched a pair of young cowboys dodging around bushes, snapping caps at each other. An old longing clutched at her and she stared at them in rapt concentration, until she heard the coffee boiling.

She lifted the cream carefully out of the refrigerator, placing it on the print cloth, beside the sugar. In the clear, cold water running from the tap, she rinsed a cup, filling it with steaming coffee. Doctored it to the proper shade and consistency, beginning the same old thought reactions that always coursed her mind, whenever she had a quiet moment.

Why had she never conceived? That was the crux of the entire problem. Maybe because she wanted a child too much? Could that be? They had been as intent on conception, after their marriage, as they had been careful to avoid it, before. She had given in to Ken, when she was sure he was going to marry her; possibly too often, but she thought not. A fellow gets tired of a girl he thinks is a push-over. She had gone all the way, just often enough to let him know that she really cared, and then only when he had served, what she termed, his apprenticeship. After all, they had gone steady, over a year, going out once or twice a week. He had made a little more progress each time, until, finally, one night, she found that she couldn't wait any longer either.

It was funny, thinking back on it now, how secretly frightened she had been. In those sweet, innocent days, she had believed, and so had most of the other girls, except some in school who lived a dark, secret life of their own, that you only had to do it, and maybe not all the way, but just touch a boy in a certain, unknown way, and you were finished. You might as well be dead, because everybody would know that very minute, and you would have a baby, and you would have to go away, and that was the end. Anyway, that's what mothers said.

How green she had been. She needn't have worried.

There never had been anyone else in her world, but Ken. Sometimes, it had been better to make him think otherwise, that there was someone else looming big on her horizon, but it had always been a big joke, and no matter how hard she had tried to fool him, he had always known it.

Their wedding was in June, one of the first after graduation, and the Lawrence's and her folks had paid for two weeks in San Francisco, and they'd had two weeks in a cozy, tiny room in a hotel, she'd forgotten which one years ago, and they hadn't been careful or anything, but just let everything fly and the devil with it all. It was a wonderful thing, then, to have such control over a huge man like Ken, to be able to wring him out and make him weak as a kitten, when it was all over and you were lying beside him, mothering him, like he was your first born, and all the time, you were as strong and ripe as all the tigers in the jungle.

It made her tingle, even now, just to be sitting here, alone, a single lazy fly humming against the wall in the late afternoon sun, just thinking how it had been.

They had really tried after the honeymoon; sometimes frantically, because they felt the world creeping up on them, lying quiet, ready to pounce. They had a tiny apartment, not far from her mother's, because her folks had been nice to them and she missed them a lot, until the army took Ken.

They had married too late, they were born too young, he had said. They had waited too long, he told her that night, and in the morning it was raining when they drove to the station.

There had been long nights of tight fists clenching a handkerchief, wet with tears, of staring into the darkness, searching her thoughts for certain meanings she couldn't find. It had been terrible. She was lost, living with her mother again, having to swallow that saccharine sympathy from her people, whom you knew were glad that all this had happened, because now they had their own sweet Connie back again. In their minds, you were still an unsullied virgin who had never been touched by vile man.

If she had only had a child then, to show them the proof that she was also a living, desiring and desirable woman.

And every night, tossing and turning in her bed, waiting for the fires of awakened passion to ebb and die away, after writing her nightly letter to Ken, torturing herself with thoughts of how it had been, and how it could be right this moment, if it wasn't for a few paranoic leaders in this cracked and crazy world.

How could such a thing happen? And why? Just when you were discovering the potentials of this marvelous body of yours. Experimenting with strange appetites and their marvelous antidotes.

It was maddening to sit brooding in the house, day after boring day, and you were being eaten up by nerves and frustration, until one rainy Monday, you went out of the creaking front door and got yourself a job at Douglas, on an assembly line, making landing gear for bombers.

Slugging your heart out, day by day, counting your memories, wishing he were home. Your whole life made up of dreams. Believing that the harder you worked, the sooner Ken would be home. What a fallacy.

You never imagined a war could be so drearily long, stretching into a never ending infinity. You discovered another thing that you hadn't dreamed possible. That your love for Ken had possibly been too intense, too all pervading, like leather blinders on a horse. The blinders themselves, might be of the best quality leather, but they never let the horse see anything but the road ahead. And love was like finger tracings in the dust. The winds of time blurred the markings so that finally, you could hardly read the original writings. As time passed, more and varied activities came to have an important place in your life, and the white heat of passion gradually cooled.

And so had the coffee. With a shudder, she ground her cigarette into the saucer. She stood quickly, crossing to the stove, pouring herself another cup. She wished Gladys hadn't called, starting her off on this long trail of introspection.

As she slowly stirred the sugar in her cup, she reflected that it wasn't like her to be so pensive. She had killed that off long ago. Now she was the live wire of committees and clubs. She had fought hard for this detached, amused air she affected. When Ken was away, she had substituted social endeavor for the sex urge that had threatened to destroy her so many times. Working in the plant, pretty, alone, the way she was, she had gotten the rush from plenty of men. She could have had any kind she wanted. They were much older than she, in most cases, well established, with all kinds of money, if that had been her aim. She learned to turn them away, with a smile and a fast, light word.

Until Rich.

Her heart gave a tiny jerk when she thought of him. All that had been so long ago. When was it? '43? No, it had been the spring of '44, nearly two years ago, because Ken had just been transferred from North Africa to some big camp on Salsbury Plain in England, and she remembered being so relieved to think him out of danger. Never dreaming they were saving him for Omaha Beach.

Rich was like all the rest at first. Just a joke. A guy that came around, teasing you, hiding your lunch, or asking you how you were making out under the weight of the torch you carried. There were a million of them, and you never paid much attention. You laughed along with them and forgot it.

You never dreamed he was serious, until Gladys brought it up in the rest room, during a break.

"I think Rich has it bad." She shook her fluffy blonde head, as she ran a comb through her hair, cigarette poking from the corner of her tight mouth.

It was a small department and everyone on the line had their nose in someone else's business.

"Has he?" you said, knowing why the cat would bring it up. Not believing it, because you were sure you'd never given him the slightest break.

"And how. It bulges out all over."

If you were to be absolutely honest with yourself, it did bring a certain glow to your body, thinking Ken wasn't the only man you could bring to a slow boil. But that was nothing to be thinking of, and you thrust it from your mind.

"You're kidding, of course. He just likes to goof around. He doesn't mean a thing by it."

"Now you're the one that's kidding. Kidding yourself. You think the whole thing's a joke? Have you ever seen Rich laugh, when he's goofing around? Because he's looking right into your eyes all the time."

"You don't know what you're talking about. You're crazy."

"Is that right? You just check up on it, the next time he comes around and see if little Galdys has popped her wig."

And you found that she was right, and though you secretly fought it, the fact remained that you were glad. Rich grinned the easy smile, joked and laughed with you, but his large, dark eyes were fastened solemnly on your own all the time. Checking your reaction; seeing how everything went over. Even in the bowling alley.

The plant, in order to maintain a closer relationship between foreman and line-bucker, had sponsored a bowling league that met in the Sunset alleys every Wednesday night. Connie looked forward to this evening every week, with anticipation, because this was the only recreation she allowed herself. Her conception of being true to her husband was to shut herself away from all the social joys of metropolitan Los Angeles and vicinity, in the manner of an ascetic. She worked her eight- or ten-hour day, with a certain amount of joy and rapt concentration, returning home bone weary at night, to eat a silent meal with her parents, both of whom she resented very much at this time, and spending the remainder of the evening pouring out her stifled passion in erotic love letters to Ken.

After Gladys had underlined Rich's interest in her, she became more and more conscious of him. She seemed to see his deep, dark eyes on her wherever she went. And there was something about the pounding racket of the bowling alleys that seemed to heighten the pressure of the pulsing blood in her veins. One Wednesday night, she purposely looked across to the alley he was using. Their eyes found each other, and for a long moment, their glances locked. She forced her head away and stared at the floor, ashamed.

What the hell was the matter with her? Some of the well remembered tingling had scratched through her outer nerves from the cap of her skull all the way down the furrow of her back. There had only been one man that had made her go all a-tremble like that, and he was thousands of miles away.

She was full of sick resolve for a few minutes, and then, in spite of herself, her eyes strayed again. After all, was she a baby, a schoolgirl, afraid to look at a man? She was emotionally mature, she told herself; capable of handling a simple situation like this. She had to see him again, to try to divine his thoughts. She would know when to quit. She was old enough to know that much.

And he was so cute, the hard muscles in his arms and chest bulging against his skin tight T shirt, his biceps making tight bands of his short sleeves. His jaw was square and large. Rich might be of Italian descent, his skin was so dark, his hair, black as night.

Suddenly, someone tapped her shoulder, awaking her from her dream.

"Get with it, Connie. It's your frame."

She had pulled her eyes away from Rich with a visible effort, like sucking a foot free of a marshy bog. She was making a fool of herself, she decided. He would have a good laugh with the other fellows over this silly, moon-struck girl. She rubbed her fingers absently around the chalk bowl. She should never have permitted herself to be part of a spectacle like that, to be carried away. She, of all people, who had always been aloof and prided herself on her poise. She had responsibilities to Ken. She had put herself into a dangerous position. A thing like that could cause malicious gossip at the plant and make her job unbearable. Pulling the towel through her hand, she scanned the racked balls for her number.

But Rich could fill a need that had gnawed at her for months. She would have to fight this impulse.

Connie made her approach, and as soon as the ball left her fingers, she felt it was wrong. It hooked too far left and picked up six and ten. She flayed her mind clear of everything but the straight, hardwood alley stretching ahead of her into the bright blaze of lights, with eight bone-white pins glaring a challenge to her from the end of it. And waited patiently for the black sphere to roll back down the runway. Heedless of the laughter behind her.

Her second ball was just a hair to the left of No. 1, and the impudent pins were spinning against the backboard, and she could see the legs of the pinboy leaping frantically clear. Her heart soared with the spare, as she turned, picking a burning cigarette out of the ash tray at her side.

Until she saw Rich, sitting easily among the other girls, obviously waiting for her to return, and she knew that everyone else was aware of it too.

You've done it now, Connie girl, she told herself.

The worst part of the situation was that she hadn't quite decided whether to nip the whole thing off right now, before it got started, or to dangle him a little. Which was powder room parlance, meaning: keep him jumping through the hoop. But would she have the will power it would take to hold him off, to bluff him away with a smile and a bright, witty saying, when the crucial moment came. Because he had that exciting devil-may-care glint in his eyes that meant he had had his way with plenty of women, and if you weren't going to play, according to his rules, he would chuck you over, and that would be that. He wouldn't waste much time, she knew; he'd get to the point quick. She didn't intend going all the way with him, but he might be the very reaction she needed. To match wits with this virile hunk of male.

She sat down beside him. Might as well make it look good for the gallery. He handed her a bottle of beer he had been holding; the chill dew on the outside of the bottle was wet against her hand.

"Drink up," he smiled.

The air felt strained. Connie felt that he was trying to say something, but couldn't quite get started. She would give him every opportunity.

"Thanks." She took a sip from the bottle, handing it back to him. "You rolling three hundred tonight?"

"I'm lucky if I can pick off a spare."

"What is your particular problem? I've never known you to have much trouble on the alleys."

"It's not the alleys that are giving trouble," he said, taking a quick, gulping swallow of beer.

"No?" Her rising inflection was a provocative invitation, in spite of herself.

"I was sitting over there, watching you, thinking how pretty you looked in your blouse and slacks, and I couldn't keep my mind on the game."

"I suppose you know that flattery will get you nowhere, my man."

"Shut up, Termite, don't interrupt. I was thinking we might take in a show, or a drink or something, after the league is over."

She dropped her eyes to the floor, and then hated herself for doing it, recognizing it for a sign of weakness, when she needed to be strong.

"I couldn't," she said.

"Why not?" Her hesitation had given him courage to pursue the point. "What else have you to do?"

"I have to go home and write a letter to my husband. He's overseas." Simply, as though this would erase the whole problem.

"Okay, so we know you're married. Don't be so damned prim. I'm not asking you out because I want to make wild love to you. I like you. You're a good kid. I like to have you around for laughs."

"I don't feel much like laughing."

"That's why you need to go out more than you do. To get away from yourself. Cooped up inside four walls, day after day, is enough to drive anyone crazy. C'mon, Connie, let's get out of this flea trap after the league, have some drinks and dance. What do you say?"

"On one condition."

"Anything you say."

"That I'm in by midnight, and my girl friend, Gladys, comes along." She couldn't depend on will power alone. She had to have some insurance.

"Holy Canarsie! That's two. And what are we going to do with the extra girl?"

"That's your problem."

"She can go along with my buddie. We'll make a double date out of it. But why do you want her tagging along? You Siamese twins, or something?"

"You said you weren't going out with me to make love. I'm just making it easier for you to keep your promise."

"I didn't promise anything," he said, sullenly.

Connie felt a quick spasm in her chest, as she saw the mock pout on his lips. It so reminded her of Kenny. It was a thing that he would do.

She laughed. The world was opening up for her again. It had been so long since she had felt she was wanted.

"You'd better promise, if you want me to go," she frowned, and made as if to go.

"Where you going?" he asked, a strand of his jet hair falling across his forehead. He looked up into her face.

"To tell Gladys we're going, as soon as you promise not to make a pass."

"How about if I promise just for tonight?"

"Well...okay."

They found a smoky little hole in the wall, north of the Strip, and drank vodka. Collins for the girls, and the men had it straight, with water on the side. They sat, side by side, the four of them, in a horseshoe shaped, leather booth, mostly talking shop. A piano, bass, guitar and drums pumped out a slow beat, and couples danced in the dim mist that shrouded a pocket-sized dance floor.

"Old Larry's about the fastest guy I ever seen on a drill press," Rich said to his friend.

"He's fast all right, and he gets out production. But he takes chances. What good's production, after you've lost a hand?"

"You're right there, Buddy. Best thing to do is set a pace, fast enough so as to not get your stuff out too fast, if you get what I mean. The whole thing is, it's a thankless damn racket. The more you do, the more they expect you to do. No use killing yourself for a stinking buck and a half an hour."

Connie turned to him, eyes blazing. "Don't you want this war to end?" she said intensely. "Don't you want the boys to come home?"

"Now don't get your water hot, Baby. Do you think that I, personally, can make even one rear rank private come home a second sooner? This war will be over when the big boys, the industrialists, politicians, and all the rest of the big wheels, the ones you and I never see or even hear of, think they've scooped enough money off the top. When they scoop all their greenbacks into a vault and sit back and wait another ten or twenty years until they have enough munitions, planes and other junk in their stockpiles to furnish both sides with materials for another war.

Then they'll start planting the hatred doctrines in the newspapers, which they own, and broadcasting the crap over the radio networks, which they also own. Wise up, Beautiful. It's all a big trap, just like everything else in this new, shiny world, and what you and I think and do, don't matter a damn as far as the war or anything else is concerned."

Connie took a quick sip of her drink.

"What kind of a warped mind have you got? What if everybody in the country felt about things the way you do? This country would be in fine shape, wouldn't it? You don't really believe that. You can't."

"Certainly, I believe it. It's true. And I'm not beatin' my brains out because your old man's in the army. I'll be right alongside him, one of these days. My deferment can't last forever. The big shots at the plant will get wise, sooner or later, that they can hire any old blister, in his fifties, with a wife and eight kids, to come in and buck rivets, eight hours a day. Or the place will be run by you gals. And Junior will be clocking his overtime in a 1944 model foxhole."

Rich shook a cigarette out of a pack, lit it, and handed it to Connie. Gladys and Frank, bored with serious conversation, were dancing on the floor.

"Do you know, Rich," Connie said, allowing the smoke to eddy from her nostrils, "that there are plenty of German agents who'd be happy to hear you say things like that. I know you don't mean it the way it sounds, but it is subversive talk. And I know that I can't accept your ideas. You must find it hard to live with yourself."

"Not at all. No more uncomfortable than it is for you, with your head stuck in that bucket of sand."

"I've got an open mind. I can see your side of the story. I've heard other fellows talk like that. Kenny used to. But you're wrong. All of you."

"If it makes you feel any better to feel the way you do, by all means go ahead. But don't get carried away. I didn't think you'd take what I said to heart. I was only needling you. Don't make such a big thing out of it."

Connie mashed her cigarette roughly into the tray. She turned away from him, staring out toward the dance floor, angry and upset. It was futile to press the point with him, because he wouldn't be pinned down. Maybe he was just making fun of her. So many men did ridicule women in an honest argument. And Rich could be so devilishly sarcastic when he wanted to. And conceited. He really loved himself. But you had to give him credit. He was exciting. You never could tell what he might say.

"Don't get sore," he said in a placating tone.

"I'm not mad. I just don't like to hear you talk about important things, as though they were all a big joke. There are some things in this world that are serious, you know."

"Want me to get you a soapbox? And pass a plate?"

"Okay, I'll shut up," she said, sheepishly. "I can never tell when you're kidding."

Rich gripped her hand hard, his forehead wrinkling into a shape of concern. Her defense mechanism, weakened from the dispute, allowed her heart a huge gasp of pleasure.

"I don't want to fight with you, Beautiful," he said, softly. "Believe me, no matter what I say to you after this, I won't be kidding."

Now was the time for a strategic withdrawal, she told herself. It was hard to be a hypocrite, by going coy, like a simpering schoolgirl, but she must.

She pulled her hand back gently.

"Don't lose your head. Remember your promise."

"You can't get shot for trying."

"All depends for what."

They sat in silence a moment, watching the dancers moving rhythmically through the smoke. The set ended, and a waltz group sang around their ears.

"You want to try one?" Rich asked.

"I'm kind of tired. Maybe a slow, easy one. Okay?"

"Anything you say, Beautiful. It's your party."

He was light on his feet, as she knew he would be. She fitted into the tight circle of his arms, and he held her masterfully, piloting her around the tiny floor, dodging other dancers with ease and skill. It was wonderful to feel the warmth of him seeping through the layers of her clothing. Allowing her strong, young breasts to flatten, ever so slightly against his massive chest.

As they danced, Rich held her tighter and closer, and their hips swayed in the rhythm of the music. He was doing something with his leg, so that it pushed against her, but his arm held her so hard against the small of her back, that she couldn't do anything about it. She stiffened a little, trying to pull away. Not a muscle moved on Rich's face, as she scanned it for possible disappointment.

She knew he desired her, wanted something from her, she dared not think about. It stood to reason, because at this short acquaintance, what other basis could there be for extended companionship. True love is based on shared experience. That stuff about being a good kid, along for laughs, was seed for the birds.

That was the trouble with men. They always treated you as though you were a nine-year-old child.

"Nice?" he asked, his face close to hers.

"Nice."

She allowed him to take her hand, leading her back to the table through the milling dancers. Gladys was fidgety.

"Let's get out of this fly trap," she piped. "Tomorrow's a work day, and I have a hard enough time, as it is, getting out of bed in the morning."

"You mean to go home?" Frank asked.

Connie knew that certain arrangements had been made, because Gladys didn't flare up, like she usually did. She just grinned at Frank, pretending that nothing had been said.

Connie felt she would have to tread softly now. Gladys wouldn't back her up, if she got into deep water with Rich. Frank would probably be manipulating her in the back seat, and Gladys wouldn't care about anything else. She would be passionately engaged in the precarious practice of eating her cake, while keeping it safely locked away.

It was time to fish, or cut bait.

"It's all right with me," she said. "I'm ready to go, if everyone else is."

"C'mon, fellow slaves." Rich led the way. "Let's get into those beds, grab a few winks, so we can get back to the salt mines in the morning."

Connie watched, as Frank and Gladys stood together for a long time, facing each other. Frank placed one hand on each of the blonde's buttocks and pulled her close. She stifled her revulsion as she realized that Gladys didn't have anything to lose. She was single, had no ties, and if she followed the simple rules of feminine hygiene, there was no reason in the world why she shouldn't have a good time for herself tonight.

For herself, it was different. After you had been loved by a man like Kenny, even the most attractive, handsome men, gave you nothing more than a passing thrill. That was why she was so positive she could handle anything that came up with Rich. It would be fun to experiment to see if his love-making came close to Ken's. But no, on second thought, she had too much to lose. She would tease Rich to a certain point, and then insist that he take her home. She couldn't afford to do anything else. One slip, and her whole life would be thrown away, ruined. Besides, Kenny deserved something better than this. What if he could see her now? Sitting in this cheap little bar, with a fellow that obviously wanted her for just one thing. How had she brought herself to do a thing like this?

The evening had gone flat, like beer standing in an open bottle in the sink.

She took Rich by the hand, leading him out. Let Frank and Gladys follow, if they wished.

"Let's go, if we're going."

"Don't be in such a rush," Rich said.

"I want to get home. I've got tons of things to do, before I can go to bed."

It was damp, chilly, in the wide expanse of the parking lot, and there was a trace of fog coming in from the sea. Rich opened the front door of the Mercury, and she slid into the seat. She watched his lithe grace with pleasure, as he crossed in front of the car, opening his door and getting in beside her. With a deft movement he flicked the radio button on the dash.

Frank and Gladys were not in sight.

Rich turned toward her quietly, staring into her eyes, resting his warm hand on her leg.

"What's the trouble, Beautiful? You're scared to death of me, aren't you?"

"No. Why should I be? What makes you say that?"

"Because you want to rush right home. With convenient reasons for doing so, that you just made up."

"I didn't make them up." Her voice faltered, as she felt the warmth of his hand, through the light material of her slacks. It set up a delicious trembling that she hoped he wouldn't feel.

"The hell you didn't," he said, tightening his hand.

He slid closer to her on the seat, handing her a cigarette. They listened to soft, dreamy music, as they smoked.

She could see Rich watching the rise and fall of her breasts in the dim light, as she smoked quietly. It pleased her somehow, to know that she had the power, still, to tempt men. It had been a long time since she had consciously tried.

"Sometimes," Rich said, suddenly, "I feel like taking this Merc and filling it full of gas some morning, and just head out. Drive north or east or any place, till I run out of gas. Stay there awhile, until I get tired, and then do it again. Anything to get away from this dead routine.

"I know what you mean."

Rich inched closer, sliding his arm along the back of the seat, above her shoulders. She felt a sense of contentment, knowing that his strength was in back of her. Then she tensed a little, feeling impending passion, knowing conflicting emotions, anticipation and dread, at the same instant.

"You must lead a hell of a life," he said, sympathetically. "No recreation, no fun. What do you do with your spare time?"

"I don't really have much," she said. "I keep busy most of the time. Helping Mother around the house, doing odd jobs. I keep busy."

"Oh, you live at home."

"Disappointed?"

"Kind of."

His arm slipped around her shoulders, and he cradled her against his heavy muscles. She welcomed him as a refuge, and said nothing. At least, he was frank about everything. A certain wildness engulfed her, giving her the feeling that she could do as she liked with this brute. She had him classified, she decided. A rampaging, male brute—and it was exciting.

"You poor kid." Rich bent to look into her face in the high moonlight. "What do you do for loving? A girl as pretty as you are, that's been married and everything. What do you do?"

"Not everything," she laughed, "just married."

"No kidding. How do you stand it?"

The few drinks she had had were beginning to make her head spin.

"Stand what?" she asked, inanely.

"Who loves you the way you need to be loved?"

"Nobody. And what makes you think I need to be loved?"

"I just know, that's all. A girl with a heavy, passionate lower lip like yours, needs a lot of the old loving to keep her going."

"You know too much. Or, at least, you think you do," she said, admitting her defeat, but leaving a loophole of escape.

Maybe that was what was wrong with her lately, she thought. Maybe a little wouldn't hurt. Just so she didn't let it go too far. She wasn't going to be a push-over for black, wavy hair, and a few muscles.

She allowed herself to relax a tiny bit more against his arm.

"That's where you're wrong, Mr. Rich," she said. "I can last until Ken gets back."

"Can you?" he said.

She saw him smile in the near dark, as he put his index finger under her chin, lifting her face toward his, despite her will to stop him, and though her resolve was strong, somehow, she couldn't stop him and he was closing her in, crushing her breasts against his hard, knotty chest, and even though it felt good to be crushed again, she couldn't stop him even though she meant to try but somehow she couldn't, and he was bruising her lips with his and she could feel the stubble of his beard abusing her face.

She struggled weakly, but she was held rigidly against him by his strong arms. One of his large hands was pressing between her shoulder blades, pushing her brassiere snap into her flesh, controlling the pressure of her breasts against his chest. Tightening and loosening the tension so a certain stimulating, pulsing motion was put into effect which was not unpleasant. The other hand was at the base of her spine, trying, she knew, to force her hips against his in a dress rehearsal of the act he hoped to accomplish.

Her breath surged in her burning lungs, rising again and again like huge irridescent bubbles that threatened to burst. It was delicious to be kissed in this fashion, to be enfolded, smothered, lost in this crushing strength that left room for only one thought in her swirling brain. In the first few seconds of the kiss, all her resistance vanished, and she allowed her arms to slip around his neck in suppliance.

He broke his lips from her suddenly, burying his face into her neck. Working furiously, like the craftsman he was. The quick release of her searing breath made her breasts heave, and she cringed as his fingers gouged into them, cupping them savagely.

She strained away from him weakly. Had she gone too far already?

Rich was sighing repeatedly in her ear, causing shivers to run along her spine, her thighs to quiver at the roots. She pressed herself closer to him, their lips meeting again.

"Don't Rich, don't," she sighed, softly. "You musn't do this."

She tried, but it was no use. She was weak, and after a few flaming kisses that ate into the marrow of her bones, his rough hand was caressing her elsewhere. Her world was spinning madly, and the only force she recognized was that of Rich's heavy mouth.

Finally, she pushed his hand away, holding it at arm's length.

"No, Rich," she gasped. "You promised."

"To hell with promises."

He bent to his work again.

"You can't do this. I won't let you."

"Yes, you will."

He fondled her skillfully, forcing her body close. Their hips met, and she could feel the burning warmth of his body through her light clothes. Rich fumbled at the neck of her blouse, intent as a small boy vivisecting an alarm clock. She suspected nothing until she felt his flesh on hers, his hand slipping tightly under her brassiere, his fingers pinching her hard nipple.

With a tremendous heave, she popped his hand out of the top of her blouse, like a cork out of a bottle.

"No. Stop it," she breathed.

Rich was not diverted nor put aside so easily. He let the outcast hand slip around her, slide up the muscled furrow in her neck. Boring his mouth into hers with another kiss. Connie knew that Rich suspected that her will was weakening. Her breathing gave her away. Why was it that women were always so weak and pliable? A pair of experienced hands playing a certain tune on her body could produce any degree of emotion they desired.

Gently, and ever so slowly, Rich pulled the tail of her blouse out of her slacks, keeping her attention directed elsewhere with the harassing action of his lips and other hand. By kisses and manipulations. When this phase of the operation was completed, he cautiously slipped his hand up her bare back and worked the catch of her brassiere until it slipped free. Connie was amazed when the tightened restraint on her breasts fell away.

Before she could open her mouth to protest, Rich's hot, moist hands were up and under, covering. Pulling her into a kiss, and the delicious warm syrup that was her blood now, was rising into her head and it threw certain thoughts into the foreground of her brain; thoughts she hadn't had for over a year, and now she welcomed them like old friends.

"Why?" She felt sultry, possessed.

"They're too beautiful to keep locked up like that."

She felt she should struggle away, if her heart wasn't in it. For convention's sake, if nothing else, and her weakening resolve sent the message sluggishly through the nerve channels to her brain. Then Rich kissed her again, and all communication stopped for the moment. When he released her for a moment, she tried again.

It was useless. His leg was covering her own, and when she moved back and away from him, she only succeeded in lying flat on the seat. But it didn't matter, she told herself drowsily, she was more comfortable anyway.

Rich followed his advantage, moving in to kiss her again, his body crushingly on top of her, gripping, massaging, mumbling in her ear. He began to fumble with the buttons at the top of her slacks.

"Please—please don't," she gasped, pushing his hand away.

"Don't be silly." He leaned over her in the dark, his voice scarcely more than a soothing whisper. "You need this as bad as I do. Don't kid yourself."

"No. No. I can't."

She twisted away from his descending mouth. She was battling her own traitorous will to do this thing, because her blood was fire itself, banked in her veins.

Rich's hair fell in wiry strings across his forehead, and he held her flat by sheer weight. His hips had caught hers in their pulsing flight and pressed them to the resilient seat. One of his cruel hands crushed her breast, bringing wonderful pain, and the other gripped her shoulder.

She was all but nude, from the waist up, her wispy blouse covering very little, the dragging brassiere functionless without the all important clasp. Connie was afraid that Frank and Gladys might find them, if they came out to the car suddenly. She welcomed the consummation of the scene they were playing, she admitted to herself. There would be no stops tonight. She gave no thought to the consequences, she just dreaded being caught. To be interrupted, compelled to share the secret with someone other than Rich.

He took his hand from her shoulder and forced her lips to meet his own. Roughly, he tried to insert his tongue between her lips, and this revulsed her. It cheapened everything, making it seem brassy and rancid. She closed her teeth tightly against his advance, and with a quick snap of her head, forced her mouth free of him.

"Stop it, Rich. Quit it right now." She heaved up, trying to rid her body of his crushing weight. It was useless.

"Why should I?"

"Because this has gone far enough. Too far."

"Has it?" he mocked. "Don't kid yourself. You like what I'm doing to you and you know it. I like what I'm doing. Why should I stop?"

"Because Gladys and Frank will be out here in a minute. What will they think?"

"Don't you think that if they were coming back here, they'd have turned up an hour ago?"

"Where are they?"

"I gave Frank a message. He took Gladys home in a cab."

His conceit hit her like a blow in the face. She felt her emotions swept clean away, as though doused by cold water. What a complete Grade A stooge she had been. From the beginning, he had regarded her as a push-over. And she very nearly had been. He had never considered her from any other angle, except the utility one. For just one purpose, and that was all. One idea had been in his rotten mind all the days at the plant. He'd put on an act, appearing serious, because he was smarter than all the others. It had worked up to a certain point.

This place, right now, was the parting of the ways. From now on, they would be working in opposite directions.

How had she come to be such a sucker, drinking in his line like mother's milk, enthralled with every word he said. Surely she wasn't that starved. Something to hold on to in this drifting world? Possibly, but she thought not. Sensing that her life was sifting through her fingers and would be gone, before she had had time to appreciate it? Probably, but at any rate, something was the matter with her emotions. She would never be able to trust them again.

She breathed a silent sigh of relief as she realized how closely she had come to complete submission. In her mind, she thanked Rich, because in his arrogance, her eyes had been opened.

She knew that Rich considered the battle won, the conquest finished. All that remained, was to collect the victor's spoils.

Well, she had news for him.

She asked herself which would be the easiest way to get out of this awkward and unbearable position. Rich practically had her now. He had unzipped her slacks and they had fallen away from her stomach, and she felt his hand caressing the bare midriff, below her breasts, now devoid of sensation. A few moments back, this action might have been welcomed breathlessly, sending her into ecstasies of joy. Now, it left her cold, even revolted her.

But the fact remained. There was little time to lose, if she was to make a positive move.

Her voice came, hard, flat—a monotone.

"That's quite enough. Get up."

He paid no attention. He slid his questing fingertips down further, moving his hated lips against her thigh. It did nothing to her.

For an instant, as Rich shifted his position, she found just enough space between them to bring her knee sharply into the pit of his stomach. He grunted, relaxing his grip on her, and she struggled away. He gripped her breast tightly with a free hand, trying to force her back under him again. She wrenched away in fury.

"Turn me loose. Let me up," she shouted, with venom in her voice.

"What's the matter?" Rich mumbled.

Connie could almost see the wheels clicking in his brain. He was stunned. His goal, almost reached, when he had her emotions reeling, when he had her almost pleading with him to continue—and then she had to pull this stunt.

"I want to go home," she said, coldly.

She watched the flame spread in him. He started away from her, boiling.

"You goddamn teasing son-of-a-bitch. You're afraid to go. Your kind likes to get a guy all stirred up, so you can get your pleasure, then leave him holding the bag. You cheap little whore."

She had expected this. She had asked for it. Actually, he couldn't have been farther from the truth.

She straightened, leaning back against the door. She could give him a little back.

"I should be kicked in the head for not seeing through you before," she said. "I don't care what you think, and I don't have to account to you for what I think. I just want to go home."

"I ought to lay you right here and now. Take it from you by force. But I don't want a rape charge hanging over my head—you—you son-of-a-bitch."

His language flayed her. No one had ever talked to her like this. The sewer filth that spewed from his lips had quickly turned an idyllic interlude into a nightmare—a horrible thing, filled with shame and hatred. She had only herself to blame. This was payment for being a complete fool. She would never again permit her defenses to drop so that she found herself trapped, with her back against a wall, as she did right now.

"You'd never have the nerve," she said, with false courage.

Rich never spoke another word to her.

He squirmed under the wheel in mute rage, jamming the ignition key into the lock, grinding the starter, until the engine kicked over. They swirled through the deserted streets at a speed they could have clocked in the time trials at Indianapolis. Connie felt that Rich wanted to be rid of her as quickly as possible, even if he had to kill her to do it.

She didn't care, one way or the other. She was deeply ashamed, and remorse swept over her in succeeding black waves.

Ken, Ken, she thought. What must you think, away off there, in the other world you live in. Tell me how I came here. How I could do a thing like this. I'm unclean, grimy, a thing to be cast aside. Why am I here, with this thing that has the shape of a man? Sometimes, Ken, you are lost and will accept anything for a substitute. As though this wolf by my side could ever be compared to you, my love. If you were only here to protect me from myself. What good are dreams, hopes, visions, when all I need is you.

Rich slammed to a stop before the darkened bowling alley, reaching across her to open the door before the car stopped rolling. As though he were ridding himself of some vermin. Connie got out with a sigh, turned her back, and stalked off without looking back. She smiled as Rich clashed gears, digging away from the curb.

She turned the corner, and there, in the harsh light of the street lamp, was her old Ford. It was like meeting an old friend in a strange town. It brought a warmth to her that she needed, a touch of home. It had been Ken's for so many years, and then it had belonged to both of them.

She unlocked the door and slid under the wheel, lovingly patting the scarred dashboard. This was better than a new Mercury any day.

After she had had time to calm down and give the matter some thought, she was afraid that Rich might give her some trouble at the plant. Spread stories, rotten lies about her to some of the other fellows. She would hate to be a rest-room prostitute. He might even try to get her in bad with the foreman, out of spite.

But she was safe on that score. Rich left her completely alone, as though she was the bearer of a plague.

In the months that followed, Connie had herself appointed to a score of committees, burying herself in social activities. Things that could keep her mind from thinking along other, more dangerous channels. Groups that avoided personalities. Recreation committees in all variations. Chairman of the dance committee, getting up a picnic, collecting for funeral donations, even down to the annual checker tournament.

And after this, she still had too much time to think. Time to stay home, having her parents spew their pulpy sentiments over her. She was driven to still other activities. She taught a Sunday school class, handling tots of three and four, loving every minute of it. She attended meetings on Sunday nights with young people of her own age. There were several of them, young, married, their husbands overseas, with the tight-drawn look of frustration in their faces. Connie organized them, forcing their desires into other paths.

They met twice a week in each other's houses, playing bridge, gossiping.

And just when Connie, through months of concentrated effort, had gotten all of her substitutes for loneliness, all of her antidotes for the sexual urge, lined up and in order—every spare moment occupied, attaining the stage in psychological adjustment to the point where she didn't require dreams of a vanished husband to sustain her any longer, Ken came home.

It was a Wednesday night, and though Connie had dropped the bowling league from her curriculum, tonight, she and a group of women were giving a shower for an expectant mother.

Her mother was following a great detective through his final maze of logic, on the radio, when the telephone jangled. She snatched at two or three more lines of the drama, before she rose, lips pursed in aggravation. Father was in his shop in the garage, turning on the lathe, or she would have made him answer the pesky thing.

"Yes?" she asked, eager to go back to the detective. It had taken him such a long time to discover what she had been sure of, since the third chapter.

The voice was dim as candlelight, whispering across the intervening miles.

"This is Ken. I finally made it. I'm home." The voice was jammed with barely restrained joy.

"Ken? Home again?"

"Yes. Wonderful, isn't it?"

"Where are you now? When will you get home?"

"I'm at Kilmer in New Jersey. I had my first steak in two and a half years."

"That's wonderful. I'll bet your people are happy."

"I haven't called them yet. I 'phoned Connie first."

"Oh, that is a shame. Connie left, not forty-five minutes ago. A shower for a friend of hers that's expecting. She's such a busy girl."

Mother Knight would never have admitted the warmth she felt as she heard the chill creep into Ken's voice. It was dead with disappointment. He had never been enough for Connie, anyway, and if the girl hadn't been so silly and headstrong, the two would never have been married.

"She couldn't stay in just this one night?" He asked no one.

"Don't be silly, Ken. How did she know that you were to call this one night, out of all the hundreds that she's been waiting. Besides Connie's a pretty busy girl. There's scarcely a night goes by, that she's not out doing something. That girl belongs to more clubs and organizations."

"I wrote her a letter about three weeks ago, telling her I was coming home."

"Yes, and she's almost delirious. Flighty as a young filly. She can hardly contain herself. She's planning a second honeymoon, as soon as you get home."

"I should be there in a few days. I picked up some late scoop on the grapevine that they're going to fly the fellows from California home. We'll probably get our discharge in Northern California someplace. You get out pretty fast now."

"That will be wonderful. You'll stay with us, until you and Connie find a place, won't you?"

"I can't decide anything now, until I've seen Connie. I'd better hang up before my money runs out. I've still got to call my folks."

"All right, Ken. We'll be seeing you."

Those days had been wonderful, especially the first few, after Ken was home and she had the feel of him once more. Connie sipped her scalding coffee in the light of the waning afternoon, and thought that now it all seemed a dream, the war and everything that had caused her so much pain. But it would never be a dream to Ken. Though he never spoke of it, it was an experience he would never forget, never, live down. In a way, everything he did now, was still a part of that same war, the soul-searing spectacle that had changed him from a boy into a man, and no matter how hard she tried, she could never adjust herself to some of those changes.

They had first begun to crop up during that idyllic second honeymoon in San Francisco. They had stayed at a little side street hotel, because he wouldn't let her touch any of the money she had saved while he was away. They had to use his winnings from the shipboard dice game, plus his one hundred-fifty dollars discharge pay. But they had gone to all the old places, that had altered so much, during the war, and they felt like people coming back to a neighborhood they had played in as children. A few of the landmarks were there, but not one familiar, smiling face was to be seen.

They had lobster on Fisherman's wharf, ate great rings of crisp, fried shrimp, dipped in golden mustard, in a tiny back room in Chinatown, drank dozens of potent Martinis, with swollen green olives slumbering in the bottom of the glass, stared, night after night, through vast windows, down to the torturous strings of dismembered diamonds, glinting in the dark, that were the night lights of San Francisco, from the gay bar that fills the top floor of the Mark Hopkins Hotel—and Connie knew that Ken enjoyed nothing—not even her body which she gave so freely.

Here was the thing she couldn't understand. Ken was never content. No matter what they were doing, he was restless, ill at ease, uncertain, looking forward to the next thrill. Oblivious to her enchantment, miles away in a world of his own. Sometimes she had to speak to him two or three times, before he would turn his head toward her.

Even in bed, in the late evenings, and sometimes, in the growing light of early morning, she couldn't force the essence of her into his soul, to possess him completely, the way she had before. Now he was a mad beast of the field, rampaging, ripping and tearing, not with her, for the supreme, heart filling joy of it, but merely because it was a need of the human body to be satisfied, therefore, get it finished, over and done with, now this minute, and then on, ever on, to something else, as quickly as possible. He gave no thought to her own tenderly nurtured desires, and she didn't tell him. She loved him and entered into his mood as best she could, even though he bruised her body badly on occasion.

His dislike for San Francisco was a tangible thing. He wasn't happy, and when he told Connie, she thought the reason a silly, petty thing.

"This is a damn sailor town," he said, as they walked the winding path by the lake in the park. "I hate a damn town like this."

"Why? What difference does it make to us, darling, if there are a lot of the Navy boys in San Francisco?"

"A dogface G.I. always hates the Navy."

"But, Ken, you're a civilian now. You're not in the army now, so what difference does it make?"

He rubbed his hands across his chin, stopping for a moment, doing all the little things that were so much a part of the old Ken, the one she loved.

"That's right, hon. For a minute, I forgot. That's a good one on me."

And he was careful not to mention it again, although she knew it bothered him.

In the same way that living with her folks bothered him. It was silly, because his people had been separated for years, and his mother had just a tiny flat that was barely room enough for her and her two Pomeranians, and Mom and Pop had so much extra space in their house, even though she would have been happier anywhere else. Pop had offered a good job with his firm, but Ken had taken a firm stand and refused. Telling Pop he would rather make his own way, and he didn't want any favors from anybody. Pop hadn't said too much, Connie remembered, but she knew he was hurt.

They had spent so much in San Francisco, that Ken had been a mad thing, until he had the money necessary for a down payment on the house. He had been only too glad of her bank account then. True, there had been a tingling excitement, watching it being built, going out to the lot in the evening, wondering how much the carpenters had completed that day. From concrete foundations, into two-by-four sidings, and the long wait while the cabinetmakers plied their art, and then one day, it was a complete house, with cute corner windows, venetian blinds, tile on the sink and a peach colored bedroom and everything. All the trimmings, and all on the G.I. bill.

Connie found it difficult to drop some of the clubs she was in, a lot of them had been around Glendale, where she had lived. But she had been quick in picking up new activities around her new home. And another thing that made it hard was that she and Ken argued about her job. He had said he was going to support her, and she wasn't going to go out to work. He didn't care how many fool clubs she belonged to, but no wife of his was going to hold a job. Housekeeping was a full time job in itself. She had countered by saying that it was sweet of him, but how did he expect to live in comfort and security, paying for a new home and all, on his pitiful salary alone.

She lit a reflective cigarette, remembering how completely he had blown up.

Part of it, she couldn't remember; most of it, she wouldn't repeat. But he had raved about how independent she had gotten, that it was a hell of a thing she hardly had time to give him a damn thought any more, having the house cluttered up with gabbling females most of the time. That she was so tied up with clubs and committees for this, that and the other abortion, that she didn't have time to look after her own home. It was a wonder, she even had the time for a roll in bed.

She had told him he didn't need to bring that into it. There was a limit, but he had raved some more, and she had shut her ears to most of it, until he slammed out of the house. Then she had waited, curled up on the couch with a book, until midnight, and it was long after she was in bed, that he had stumbled in. She had purposely laid there, with her eyes tightly shut. If he wanted to play games, he could play by her rules.

Finally, she had been forced, by the pressure that Ken brought to bear, to quit her job. And now she had nothing to do. It was an awful thing to face an entire day, stuck out in this tiny town, miles away from her mother and every other friend she had, with nothing to do. Housework gave her no trouble. She could get this little crackerbox cleaned up in an hour or two, and then have the whole dreary day to while away. If Ken would only leave the car, she could have visited her friends.

She inhaled deeply, then tapped her cigarette against the glass tray. It was just plain dull. If Ken were only here today. Tomorrow being Christmas, maybe they could reach some kind of an understanding.

There was always some part of him she never could reach. A part he kept locked away from her, and no matter how she tried, she could never find her way into that secret closet of his soul.

Maybe she was like Bluebeard's seventh wife. She might even now have the key, but she would be horrified at what she might find, once she opened the door. It might be the end of her.

If only there was something for her to do. A baby would fill her days. If only she could conceive.

Her coffee had gone cold. It was bitter, and she crossed to the sink, pouring the brown liquid down the drain, watching the children playing in the street.

4:45 P.M.

KEN STARED at the seared, weed-stained hills, dimming now in the fading sun, spinning by the dirty speckled windows of the cab, with half an ear tuned to the drunk, whining voice of Beverly. She'd been busy gnawing on the carcass of the bottle they had brought with them from Joe's. She was really feeling it.

"You said you were going to make it an all night party. I don't want to go home yet."

He said nothing. He was fed up to the teeth. She was just a tramp like all the rest. He had thought he had something better than ever before, bright, shiny, new as a fresh minted coin. His personality was always sparkling, flattering, before he made out. The girls were always beautiful, charming and witty, until afterwards. Bud was right.

But after the whole thing was over, it was a different story. Something was lacking. There was some one thing he was seeking, and no matter where he looked, it seemed that he had just missed it. It lay back on the trail he had just passed over, just beyond his grasp. It was always "better luck next time," and he had no chance of finding the talisman, because he was never quite sure what it was.

The main idea right now, was to get rid of this broad, get the hell home and see how Connie was. Why had he ever wasted time with this Beverly anyhow? The deal this afternoon would give her the only excuse she needed to simper at him with those impossible glasses.

He had played the role of an ass to perfection. She was sore, and she said:

"That's the trouble with you married guys. You got no time to play around. Got to hit and run. That's you guys all over."

"Got to keep a whole skin," he said, trying to laugh it up.

"Bunch of damn hypocrites," she mumbled, taking another swallow. "Eat your cake and keep it, too."

"What would you do?"

"Chuck the whole damn works. Have fun. Forget everything."

"Don't be stupid."

She could afford to say that. She didn't have anything to throw away.

"Who the hell do you think you are? Pompous bastard. Calling me stupid. Don't forget who's paying for this cab." She nearly fell in a heap, gesturing toward the driver. "I'll have him toss you out on your can. You can walk the hell home."

Ken turned to the window again, leaving her to the bottle. What a neurotic little honey she had turned out to be. You couldn't satisfy her one way or another. Always ready to go. Sore as a popping boil when you got your gun, and it was all over.

That cut thrown in your face about paying for the whole spread. It was true, but she had gotten what she paid for. Well, most of it anyway.

"Kenny," she cooed drunkenly, "why the hell do you have to rush home to your wife tonight? It's Christmas Eve, and little Beverly'll be all by her little lonesome."

"I can't help that."

"Don't be so bitter, Kenny. Your wife will get along all right."

"Not without me, she won't."

"You mean, you're really goin' home?"

"That's what the man said. And as soon as I can."

"Ken, you're a lousy, sneakin' son-of-a-bitch. You know that?"

"I had my suspicions. You'd'a been better off with Bud."

"That bastard. He's as no good as you are."

Beverly returned to musing over her bottle. The one true friend.

Ken felt a sudden, surprising wave of sympathy for her. What kind of a life did she have? Pushed around, handed a rough deal, since she was a kid. She had to get her kicks wherever she could find them. He reached across and patted her knee.

"I'm sorry it turned out this way, Bev. I should never have given you the pitch in the first place. Not when I've got a wife waiting at home."

"It's too late for tears," she said, moodily, "and anyway, there's nothing to be sorry about. I was the sucker. I knew what to expect, but I led with my chin anyway. You're too pretty, Ken."

"Always there with the laugh, huh, kid? I'll make it up to you some day."

"Forget it, Hon. Little Beverly belongs home in bed. Alone. This rotgut weighs a ton."

"Keep a stiff set of uppers, friend. We've still got to drop by Rocco's and pick up a package I left, and then ride all the way out to Hollywood to pick up the car."

"Okay, Pal. Just give me a shove when we get home."

Beverly tilted the bottle to her lips, and the last few drops slid down her throat with a convulsive gurgle. Rolling the window down, she pitched it into the street. Cuddled against Ken's shoulder, she was asleep before they had shot through City Terrace to enter the Freeway leading to the city.

The taxi screamed to a stop in front of Rocco's. Ken slid his arm gently from around Beverly's shoulders, allowing her to slump back against the seat. He nodded to the driver.

"Wait a second. Be right back."

There were only two drunks collapsed against the far end of the bar when he walked in. Rocco was idly waving a rag across the polished walnut, dreaming absently of unearned profit.

"Still got that package?" Ken asked.

"Just about to auction it off to these two winos."

He handed it across the bar.

"Thanks, Pal."

"Don't thank me. Thank God it was still here."

Ken laughed, going outside to the cab. He opened the door and saw that Beverly was still crumpled on the seat, her dress wrinkled above her knees, showing a stretch of flesh and silk, her thighs separated in the middle by the top of her stockings, and piquantly topped by the lace edge of her slip. It did nothing to him, and, absently, he pulled her dress down an inch or two, to prevent the driver from enjoying himself too much. She stirred at his touch, and he wondered about her condition.

He was flat broke, and their cab bill must be terrific. What if she got sore again and refused to pay the tab? He wasn't going to take a chance on being stuck with a loud drunk, when it came time to pay the fare. Even if she was asleep when they got there, how would it look if he went rummaging through her bag for the dough?

He'd be better off if he borrowed the cash he needed.

He laid the package on the seat beside Beverly, and returned to the bar.

"Back again, Rocco," he grinned, engagingly. "How about lending your old buddy ten 'til Monday?"

Rocco turned to the cash register, pushing a clanging "no sale" and slid a ten-dollar bill across the counter.

"I've got a hell of a cab bill outside, and I'm beat."

"You don't need to apologize. I know you're good for it."

Ken started, as he heard an engine roar into life. He streaked for the door just in time to see the taxi, his taxi, disappear around a corner, lost in traffic, carrying the drunken girl and Connie's seventy-five dollar Christmas present into nowhere.

Christ!

5:10 P.M.

AFTER A BATTLE with her weakening will, she pushed herself painfully up from the rough surface of the seat. The mohair bristles were harsh against her cheek. Whew! Boy, wasn't it drunk out this afternoon? She would never have had that last drink, if she thought it would hit her like this.

That goddamn Kenny. Going to ditch her like any tramp, after he had used her for what he wanted. He was nice as pie, before they got in bed. She had paid out plenty of the hard earned stuff for this afternoon, and now it was all going down the drain. She couldn't have him for keeps, she knew that. All she wanted, was to enter into his life and just be some little part of him for a while, and he had denied her even that. He had had the last laugh, the lovable bastard, stripping her of the only treasure she had to offer, and now, running back to his wife.

She would like to see the woman that had that blonde giant under her thumb. She would like to know her secret.

Kenny had let her down. She swayed on one hand, trying to balance herself, as the nausea surged in her stomach, and the walls of the taxi began to close in on her and to grow black, towering and forbidding in the late afternoon sunlight.

There's nothing worse than the dry heaves, she told herself. She knew her stomach from old, and expected them, because she had no food inside her.

She raised herself up long enough to look out the side window. She could make out the L. A. Mutual building down the street, half a block. They were parked in front of Rocco's place.

What was she doing here? How had she gotten here? Where was Kenny? Probably run home to mama already. Left her here to pay the cab fare. Wasn't that just like a man?

As if in answer to her unspoken question, she saw him come out of the bar, walking across the sidewalk toward the cab. A thought crossed her mind, more an impulse, than an organized plan of action. She would try to learn his plans, without his being aware of her knowledge. That way, she would have the drop on him, and he couldn't ditch her by surprise.

She dropped quickly to the seat, feigning sleep, the darkness swirling in quickening circles in her head.

She heard the door open, felt his hand against her thigh, as he adjusted her dress. She moved a tiny bit, as though her sleep had been disturbed. He would expect that. It made her warm inside to think that someone would pull her dress down, for a change.

She felt something laid on the seat beside her. She didn't dare open her eyes. The door was shut again with a slam. She peeked out of one eye.

She was alone again. Ken had gone to Rocco's.

He was a pretty nice guy after all. He was fairly honest for a man. He didn't keep you dangling, like a lot of guys would.

It was like a game of draw. You could draw one to a flush, and bet into a guy holding four aces pat, figuring him for two pair. Some players would raise the hell out of you and cut your throat, and another might say: "Save your money. You don't want to bet into me. I've got the lock." And spread their hand.

She'd be doing Ken a favor, if she cleared out. Give him a break. He was probably worrying now how he was going to get rid of her and her cab bill right now.

She sat up. Her eyes were heavy, sleepy, the activities of the day creeping up on her.

She tapped the driver on the shoulder.

"Let's go, pal."

"Your boy said wait."

"The hell with him. He costs too much There's a couple bucks in it, if we give him the slip."

The force of the car's drag threw her back against the seat. She stayed there, slowly closing her eyes. She was tired.

"Where to, lady?"

"Four hundred block, South Madison, Pasadena."

She felt herself drifting, and she didn't fight it. Her thoughts were swooping in and out, circling round and about, like while gulls floating, catching and riding the ever changing thermals along the sea cliffs. One moment, a thought would be before her eyes, etched on the wall of her brain, crystal clear. And then, quickly, shockingly, the thought would sweep out of her range of vision, as though it were fastened to the bottom of a huge, pendulous arm. And there it would be, far away, a spot on the horizon, blurred and dim. With the horrible, impending knowledge that someone all-powerful would ask her to describe the shape and form of it, at any moment.

She hooked her teeth over her lower lip. And was asleep.

Suddenly, there was something irritating her. She shrugged it away, but it continued, and in a minute, it was the cab driver, gently shaking her shoulder. Her glasses had slipped forward on her nose, and she adjusted them. She wriggled in her seat, composing herself and her clothes.

"Four hundred block, Miss. Where to from here?"

She pointed sleepily at a brown frame apartment house, built before the first World War. Three doors down.

"That's the one. That's home."

She paid the driver generously, and started up the steps of the house, when the driver shouted after her.

"Miss, you've left something here."

"No, I have everything I started with."

She saw him lean into the back seat of his taxi and come up with a box. She descended the steps carefully, curious.

Then it came to her. It must be the box Ken had left beside her and then rushed back into Rocco's. For another shot, probably.

"Thanks a lot." She reached for it, and carried the box gingerly up to her room. She was too tired to think about this new thing now. All she wanted was to get her clothes off and climb into that bed. She had never been as tired in her whole life. A couple hours sleep would be the answer. And then she would be able to battle the world again.

Once in her tiny bed-sitting room, she kicked off her shoes, funneled her light frock over her head. She stood, regarding herself in the mirror, for a few seconds, as she reached upwards along the furrow of her back and unhooked her bra. It was a relief to feel the pressure drop away, feeling the cool air rush into the hollows underneath. She contemplated going into the bathroom to clean up, but decided she was too tired for that. It could wait. She folded back the bed and laid down, drawing a single sheet over her nearly nude body. She wished, as she did many lonely nights, that she didn't have to lie alone, but recognized it for a silly dream, and grinned to herself in the darkening room.

In a few minutes, she dozed off.

5:15 P.M.

Hᴉꜱ ᴄʜᴇꜱᴛ ᴄᴏɴꜱᴛʀɪᴄᴛᴇᴅ, squeezing the last drop of blood from his heart. He stared, open mouthed, into space for several seconds, after the cab had disappeared into the clashing traffic.

All his dreaming, planning, scheming, shot? It sure looked like it. What the hell had come over that babe to jump like that? She must be crazy. If he had just kept that box with him.

But how the hell was he to know...? That was no excuse; he should have figured it. Any silly bitch that would cart a pint around in her purse....

This wasn't going to get it, standing here on the damn street, trying to bring the cab back by mental suggestion. He hadn't even noticed the driver's number, but then, who does?

There was really only one plan of action open. The company was shut down for the day; that cut off the personnel department and its file on employees. He would have to find someone who knew her and where she lived.

If Beverly had had enough sense to go home. And, providing she was sober enough to know the box was in the taxi beside her. What a spot.

Ken dragged himself back into the bar. Rocco, cigar in mouth, was lazily wiping the gleaming counter.

"What'sa matter? Your girl blow?"

"I don't give a damn about that. She had a suit in the cab with her. Wife's Christmas present. Cost me seventy-five stones."

"Ho! Plenty of trouble, hey?"

"Plenty. What in hell should I do?"

Rocco slid a bottle in front of him, capped with a shot glass. "First thing, have a drink. Makes you think clear."

"I've had too much of that stuff already."

"You never can drink too much. It's good for you."

"That's a crock. If I'd been on my toes, this would never have happened. If it hadn't been for that goddamned Bud, I wouldn't be in this spot. He brought the girl down here, in the first place." His voice was bitter.

"Don't ever lay off bad bets with another bookie. He furnished the poison all right. But you're the boy that picked it up and drank it."

"You're right there. I dug my own hole."

"I never seen the twist before, Ken, but maybe Bud could tell you where to get hold of her."

"That sounds good, Rocco. I'll buy it. You got Bud's address?"

"Sure. I keep a record of all my horse players. He owes me dough from back races. I never chip a man for money around Christmas time, but if you see him, tell him I gotta live too. Okay?"

Ken ran his fingers through his bright hair.

"How about that dough I asked you for? Am I still on for the ten?"

"Sure, kid. That's no gamble. That's a legitimate debt."

Rocco scribbled across a greasy slice of paper, handing it and another ten spot to Ken.

"Don't worry about the dough until you're loaded sometime. The hunt for your broad might run high."

Ken stepped out on the street to hail a passing cab. He told the driver to bust his butt getting to Hollywood, but it was several minutes short of a half hour, before he was in his own car again.

It was a time of evening that was Ken's favorite. The city, sprawling from the mountains to the sea, dirty, loud, cruel and blind, in the harsh revealing sunlight, had darkened down, hiding its filth and harsh, unfeeling mannerisms. Silencing its cries. It was a place to live again.

Ken drove west on Sunset Blvd., crammed with used car lots and hole-in-the-wall liquor stores, beauty salons, massive chain theatres, with beckoning neon eyes, super-duper super markets, and run-down cocktail bars. Nostalgically, he remembered how it had been before the war, before the armies of immigrants, the pioneers of the 1940's, began streaming west in their tired jalopies, to await the coming of the Messiah. The Twentieth Century Messiah. The Green Back Dollar Bill. There had been little two-bedroom homes, picket fences, grass, and even some trees along this stretch. Now, nothing but brick, concrete and glass.

The hell with it. He had more pressing things worrying him, than the state of the world. Whereabouts in this damn county, did that chicken live? He should have broken those silly glasses of hers, while he had the chance. What would she do when she found the suit? Would she leave it in the cab out of spite? Would she consider it a valuable find and try to keep it for herself. It wouldn't fit. Connie was a full six inches taller than Beverly.

Bud was his only lead.

He turned left on Fountain, felt the familiar surge of thrill, as he gunned down the hill by the school, swerving left on Hyperion. His engine strained as he climbed another hill. He kicked at the clutch, snapping the lever into second, as he raced to the top of a steep rise, overlooking the broad, inky Silver Lake reservoir. The water looked metal gray, in the last light of the sun. The bulbs mounted on the eight-foot, chain-link fence were snapping on, and the mirror of the water picked up a reflection of each bright spark.

Ken let the motor idle for a minute, staring off and across the city. It was a sultry night, and the lights, the cozy, golden lights from the homes, glinted in his eyes. Down there, where intelligent people were pulling up to a big supper of liver and onions, steak and French Fries, or even if it was just beans, at least they were home.

And here he was, like a big ass, up a damned hilltop, on a goose chase, not knowing when he was going to get home.

Connie wouldn't worry though. Not that she ever did. He had called her, saying he would be late.

Come on, he told himself. This isn't getting the suit back.

He put the car in gear, coasting around several turns with his foot on the clutch. Following these winding streets was like tracing the convolutions of the brain with a forefinger. After fifteen minutes of twining through switchbacks, he found the road to Bud's.

At the very top of a hill, sitting at the head of four flights of steps, was Bud's place. It was tiny, sadly in need of a coat of paint, and it huddled nakedly, in violated modesty, commanding a view of the lake and a wide sweep of city lights.

The house was dark. Not a light showing.

Ken's heart sank. But he would have to try it, after coming all this way.

He started climbing the stairs. There wasn't a breath of a breeze, even up on this hilltop, as he walked across the black porch that smelled of dead, withered ivy, clinging to the warped posts. He rang the bell, punching it viciously with a forefinger.

What a damn mess to be in.

There wasn't a whisper from the house. Or did he hear a tiny giggle just then? Sometimes, the quiet fooled you into making up your own noises.

He pressed the doorbell again. This time, he was sure he heard a scuffling just beyond the door, like gigantic mice.

Ken didn't wait this time, but leaned on the bell, until he heard the girl giggle again.

"Shut up, for Christ sake."

He smiled at Bud's shout, in spite of his trouble.

"C'mon, Stud, open up," Ken yelled through the glass of the door.

Someone scuttled to the back of the house, and then the lights snapped on. After a moment, the door opened about six inches. Bud's great, swarthy face filled the opening.

"Jesus, Ken, what do you want. You're screwing up my playhouse."

"You got all night to get into that."

"That shows you don't know. I got the bitch drunk, and now everything I says starts her on a laughing jag. It's horrible. I'd just got her quieted down, figuring I was going to make out any minute, and you, jughead, have to ring the doorbell. She's a pretty little piece too. I'll bet she's back in the kitchen, right now, busting her sides out."

"What the hell for?"

"How do I know, what for? Did you ever get on a laughing jag?"

"No, but I've heard of them."

"Neither did I, but that bitch in there can't stop giggling. Did you ever hear of anything as impossible as trying to lay a woman when she thinks the whole thing is a big joke? It can't be done."

"You think you got troubles?"

Bud opened the door wider.

"I'm not doing any good as I am. You might as well come in. I've got broad shoulders."

Ken seated himself on a sagging couch, on the far end of the tiny room.

"Thanks," he said, tapping a cigarette out of his pack and tossing it across to Bud.

"What's up with you? The last time I saw you, Beverly had you slated for a one night stand."

"That son-of-a-bitch. She's crazy."

"Crazy like a fox. What did she make you for?"

"It's long and sad. You got time?"

"So what else would I be doing?"

"After we left the motel, I went back for Connie's suit, I'd left at Rocco's. I came out, put it in the cab, and then went back to hit

Rocco for a big ten to pay the cab. I came back out, and no cab. And the suit cost seventy-five stones. Not counting the fact that I haven't a present for my wife tomorrow."

"Hell. That Beverly's no dummy. She's got herself a new suit."

"She's too small. It wouldn't fit her."

"She'll probably sell it."

"Get off my back, will you? You're no help at all."

"What do you want from me? I thought you came over to play games. Frankly, I wish you'd state your business and leave. I got things on my mind. I don't like to be an impolite host, but I've got to get that babe out of the kitchen, before she downs the rest of the hooch. What a lush!"

"You must know Beverly pretty well. You had her in the bar when I came in. Where does she live?"

"Hell, fellow, I don't know and that's the straight stuff. She was sitting at one of the back tables, when I came in. I put that play over with Rocco to give you a little come on. Then, the auditors and I sat down with her. She was nibbling at a pint she had in her purse at that time."

Ken was silent for a moment, inhaling deeply.

"Swell. That's all I need."

"I didn't mean to be rough on you, Pal, and I'm honestly sorry I can't help you. She said something about picking up that pint on Colorado Street. That could mean Pasadena, Eagle Rock, or Glendale. You might try bar hopping. But, it would probably be easier to wait until Monday morning."

Ken sighed, got up and crossed to the door.

"Well, I won't keep you from your work any more. I might as well forget about it until Monday, like you say. I wonder what I'm going to tell Connie."

"Tell her some hophead stuck a gun in your ribs and heisted you for it."

"That's the trouble with this world. There's too many smart people in it."

"The chaplain's tent is just down the road, Buddy. He'll punch your card."

"Let me stay awhile and tell your girl a few jokes I know."

Bud raised his fist in Ken's face.

"Get the hell out of here. That hysterical female is about to drive me fruit now."

"Okay, pal, I'll be seeing you. Hope you make out."

"I will, if it takes all week end."

As Ken closed the door softly behind him, he heard the unmistakable sound of a woman's laugh. He smiled. Bud had his troubles too.

When he got down to the street, he sat in the car a minute, finishing his cigarette. Fastening his mind on a complete blank. He kicked off the brake, coasting down the steep hill, shifting easily in second, pulling his foot slowly off the clutch. The engine gunned into life, and he circled the lake, heading into the stream of traffic. He concentrated on driving through the welter of cars and buses, but his thoughts kept seeping through, in spite of himself.

His heart was a dry, withered husk, and there seemed no reason to do a damn thing but go home and lie on the bed, with his face to the wall. He had been anticipating the expression on Connie's face, when she opened that package. He had hoped it would do something for her, like a magic potion you used to read about, and they would be together again—really together, in their minds and souls, if there really was such a thing. The way they had been before he went away, before she found that she had no time for him.

But that was silly. How could one single suit make all that difference? Their love had just slipped out of focus, the same as a bad photograph. They were on different tracks, going in opposite directions, and neither could quite see the other.

Connie probably wouldn't be there, when he got home anyway. He'd fix himself a sandwich and a cup of coffee, and maybe, take in a show.

The never ending parade of headlights in his eyes was making him sleepy. He decided he'd be much better off in the sack, getting some shut eye.

He held the wheel steady with one hand, never decreasing his speed, and put a cigarette in the corner of his mouth. He took his eyes off the road for a split second, while he lit up.

Dammit, where was that box?

6:30 P.M.

HE SIREN whined in agony as it turned into her street, and her ears magnified the sound cruelly into her throbbing brain. For a few minutes, she clamped her eyes tight, but it didn't help. There were little men back of her eyeballs that stretched the strings in the darkness and strummed a hideous cacophony; others were spaced at intervals around the crown of her head, trying to force off the lid with mallets and chisels. Her brain swelled and shrank, with the consistency of a marshmallow. The blessing of sleep was denied her.

She sat up in bed. It was quite dark outside, and she had to stretch across, snapping on the tiny, frilled lamp on the nightstand, before she could look at her watch.

"What a head. A hell of a time to wake up," Beverly told herself.

She threw the sheet away from her legs, and swung them over the side of the bed. Her crumpled slip had worked up over her hips. As she stood up, her loosened brassiere dangled useless against her breast, feeling like a fluttering, excited hand. She leaned against the table for a moment, shrugging out of her garments, and then, when she was out of her clothes, standing smooth and creamy, she walked into the bathroom. She lathered herself carefully in the shower, taking care not to wet her hair. There was much more cold than hot water needling her naked back, and it soothed her burning skin. She stepped out, feeling a little more human.

After she had dried herself thoroughly, applying cologne to the proper places, she covered her body with a chenille robe, and went in search of food.

The chrome bones of the tiny refrigerator lay bleaching in the glare of its own fluorescent light, bare, except for the remnants of a quart of milk, a jar of olives, some shriveled cold meat, and a half bowl of soup. Beverly finished the milk, by tilting the bottle to her mouth. She was so hungry, she would have been happy with a choice cut of the south end of a north-bound horse.

If there wasn't anything to eat in the house, there was nothing to do but get dressed and go out. She knew from old, that the easiest way to get rid of a whiskey headache, was to crowd the alcohol out of her stomach with good food. She hunted around until she found her glasses.

The moment she stepped out of the bedroom, there it was. It seemed big as a house, and it hit her smack in the eye. The box lay on the first chair, inside the door, just where she had thrown it when she had come in.

"Where did that come from," she thought. "I don't remember buying anything."

When she picked it up, there was a card. She carried it over to the light. In a large, blue scrawl, she read the answer.

Kenneth Lawrence
2115 S. Hacienda Ave.
Alhambra, Calif.

Ken's box! But why did he leave it in the cab? Losing Ken at Rocco's, was the silliest thing she had ever done. He must have put the box beside her on the seat, while she had her eyes shut. She dimly remembered the driver putting something in her arms when she got out in front of the apartment house.

What a silly fool she was.

What now? She wanted to be rid of the damn thing. She had been accused of stealing before, almost put in a juvenile home, on a complaint brought by her drunken father. He was sure that one way to teach discipline to an independent brat, that wouldn't even show favor to her own dear daddy, would be to instill in her a fear of the law. She was afraid of the cops all right. She had seen the Negroes they killed, and the whites they beat up. She wanted no part of the law.

Would Ken think she stole the box? Would he be mad enough to turn her in?

She felt pressed and cramped. Suddenly, her apartment was too small, the walls closing in around her. She had to get out. What could she do?

She sat heavily in a chair, staring at the box on her lap.

A blue bolt of an idea snapped her erect. Goddamn. It was so simple, it hurt. What had happened that she couldn't think any more? She would grab a fast hamburger at the local beanery, hail a passing cab and take the miserable package back to Ken. What could be easier? The address was right there. She would be in the clear.

Why had she gotten sore and run out on Ken earlier? She was a big girl now; she should have known what the story would be. A guy that's married, can't afford to throw away his whole life for one night with a girl he hardly knows. Face it, Beverly Jean. You've been a dollar short and an hour late all your life. Ken is cute, but he's a little too rich for your blood. He'd only make you break out in a rash.

When you got the box back to him, the final curtain would be down on this little comedy.

Her morale had climbed a notch when she was outside the four walls, walking up the dark street. Things were never as bad as she imagined them. Life would continue. Ninety percent of the suicides never come off. The subject contemplates the depth of the river, the height of the bridge, and the effect of same on his clothing and appearance, and slowly melts back into the passing crowd, and is surprised at how much better everything seems, after a cup of hot coffee and an aspirin tablet.

She knew she would continue her independent plan of life, pushing against the main stream, fighting back. She needn't worry about Ken, because he wasn't available, and there were plenty of others around that could be had. That was the trouble with men. They raped so easily.

What fun would it have been with Ken anyway, even if she had given him the key to her apartment? He'd always have been jumpy, afraid of being caught. Forcing her to meet him at difficult hours in impossible places. No, it was better this way.

She gulped her food at the nearest drug store, clutching the box, between her calves, under the counter. When she had paid the bill, adding a straight ten percent of the bill as a tip, she hunted the telephone booth.

She would be glad to get rid of the damn box.

The neon lights sped by the windows of the taxi, and she watched the crowds of chattering ants in the street, and droves of their silly cars, rushing through the night to cheer friends on this mad Christmas Eve.

The night was warm, stuffy, without a breath of air. The powder between her breasts felt like putty, clammy, caked. She fluffed her blouse at the top button, to start some kind of breeze inside there, but it was useless. This was a night to be swimming in your nothings, with some fellow, in the Gulf of Mexico. But the guy she used to swim with was dead, and here she was, years later, on one of Life's dead-end alleys, hustling across a hick town.

Ten years is a hell of a long time, and you wouldn't know me now, Jerry, even if you were alive and right here beside me. I'm not the same girl at all. I'm older, wiser, and much more bitter, even though I was bitter enough that summer. I'm being used up fast. But I'll never forget that night on the beach, hunched down on the sand, with the lights of the pier in the distance, when we wanted each other so much, it was like a driving pain in our stomachs. We were so young and silly, so pathetically noble. Viewing the whole affair from the pedestal of our youth, we decided the only right thing to do was wait until we were married, and you begged me to forgive you for tearing my blouse, and ruining my stockings. If I could only have married you that moment, because there never was a more sacred time in my life. If I had only known, you'd never have gotten away with a whole skin.

Life this afternoon, wherever you are, you know all about what happened, but believe me, it is always just a substitute for what it might have been with you. All the years of happiness that a Jap torpedo cheated us of.

The cab jolted to a stop, jarring her into the present.

"This is the address, Lady." The driver turned in his seat.

"Wait here. I won't be a minute."

She decided that Ken's house was cute with the box hedge up one side of the drive and zinnias across the front. The typical home, just lacking the conventional ivy around the door.

She went up the walk, and her heels clicked across the porch. Tucking the box under her arm, her fingers pressed the doorbell. After a few seconds, she heard someone approaching the door.

7 : 0 0   P . M .

CONNIE could always hear the sound of their car, when it rounded the corner, a block and a half away. It had a distinct personality, was the possessor of a new paint job, and answered to the name of Betsy. Due to a fractured water pump, its most recognizable sound was a spasmodic light grinding of metal. And when the engine was hot, the tappets were like so many cackling geese.

Tonight, Connie was surprised when she heard the mumbling rattle of the car. Ken had said he would be in late, when he left for the office. She had accepted it without a word. Sometimes she wondered whether Ken was cheating, or if he actually spent his nights away from her as innocently as he made out. It had been some time since they had gotten together, and it was beginning to bother her. It made her cross and irritable, when she went without, for too long, making her acknowledge, reluctantly, the dependence of the sexes upon each other. There had been various reasons for this continence, most of them her own. Really, she was too tired, after haranguing a group of her club members, to feel adventurous. Either that, or she was asleep when Ken came home.

Just like a loaf of bread that lacks the rising yeast, their love lacked one precious ingredient that no one could put a finger on. Whatever it was had simply vanished, and they could not meet on common ground, couldn't get together and perform the one thing that would make them one.

Connie stood at the sink, letting the hot water run over her own few supper things. She placed them slowly in the rack to dry. As Ken rolled up the incline from the street, his headlights flashed up the side of the house, across the window, burning her eyes for a second. She was wiping the last glass, as Ken came in the back door.

"I'm sorry, Ken, but I've already eaten," she said. "I didn't know you were coming. You said you'd probably stay in town late."

"I thought I would, but I changed my mind."

He was over six feet, but she stood to his shoulder, as she crossed to him, taking one of his hands in her own.

"What's the matter, boy? Someone poison your drink?"

"Nope. I just didn't feel like drinking or raising hell tonight."

"I just had the last pork chop in the icebox. There's nothing left to eat."

"That's okay. I'm not too hungry."

"If you want to buzz up to the store and get something, I'll fix it for you."

He went through into the living room, shuffling, shoulders hunched in his coat. He stood in front of the radio, toying with the dial.

"No. That's all right. Forget it."

Connie came and stood behind him. She laid a hand on his arm.

"What's the trouble, darling? What's eating you?"

"Nothing's the matter. Why should anything be the matter?"

"No reason. I just think you ought to eat something, that's all."

"I'll go up to the drive-in in a few minutes and get a 'burger. Don't worry about it. I want to sit down and think for a minute, that's all. Is that okay?"

"Sure, hon. Anything you say. I'm going out to a show with Gladys in about an hour. I didn't think you were going to be home," she apologized.

"You've got some of the silliest friends," he said.

Connie hardly knew what to reply. He was in a fine mood tonight. He'd been grumpy a lot lately. Almost as though he were looking for any excuse to pick a fight. Well, if he thought he was going to walk on her, she had news for him.

"No sillier than some of yours I've met."

"Who, for instance?"

Here was a neat trap she would have to sidestep. Ken would try to twist their conversation to put her on the wrong side of the fence. She would be on the offensive, carrying the weight of the argument, and it would be easy for him, defending his friends. A fight like this could be run into the ground. She wouldn't have a leg to stand on, as far as he was concerned.

"Drop it. I have to get dressed for the show."

Connie knew he was sorry when these quarrels came up, ending in nothing but frustration on both sides. Actually, he was no more to blame than she was. Their marriage had fizzled, and these things were the aftermath.

"There's coffee on the stove, if you want it," she said. "I made it this afternoon."

"How many times did you heat it?"

"Just twice." She went into the bedroom, saying, "It's still good."

"Probably no stronger than pure tannic acid," Ken growled.

"If you don't want it, you know what you can do."

"What?"

Connie was silent as she shucked her housedress over her head. What was bothering him? He was like an old bear, snarling at her. Something had hurt him; he was in some sort of trouble. He couldn't keep a thing like that from her, she knew him too well.

"Go uptown and buy one," she smoothed. "They serve a good cup at the drug store."

"Okay, I'll go, if you don't want me around."

This had gone far enough. Clad in bra and panties, she strode purposefully into the living room, to the couch where he sat. He straightened in surprise, when he saw her, and she seized the opportunity to plump herself down on his lap. Her long, dark hair fell like a raven's wing across his cheek, and her breast nuzzled him, as she bent to kiss his lips.

"Now, now, Ken. Why the frown?" She smoothed the wrinkles in his forehead with her fingertips. "This is Christmas Eve. It's a happy time. Wait 'til you see what I'm going to put under the tree for you."

There wasn't a spark of warmth in his kiss. It was done mechanically, she felt, because it was required of him.

"Sure, honey, it'll be great," he murmured.

Connie heard that bitter note again. Something or someone had dealt him a low blow today. The very fact that he was home at this hour should have told her that. The only thing that made her heart rise, was that he raised his hand, giving her breast a gentle pinch, the way he always did. She kissed him again, long and slow. Her breathing started to quicken, the way it often did when she was near him. He was so much a man. The only one to get close to her heart.

In spite of her outward reserve, which she tried so valiantly to preserve, she knew she was passionate. She was proud of the fact. She could keep her man happy, if only he would let her.

His arms tightened around her for a moment, and then relaxed. Their lips broke apart suddenly, as though he were tired of this silly game.

"You'd better hurry, if you're going to the show with Gladys. She hasn't enough steady boy friends to realize the importance of being late."

"I can stay, if you'd rather. I'll call her up and say I can't make it. I wouldn't have accepted, only you said you weren't going to be home."

"It's unthinkable. I wouldn't dream of making you miss a date with one of your girl friends."

His tone was yellow acid, and she stood up quickly. When Ken was hurt inside, his defensive shell was lashing anger that struck at anything within reach. She knew that, but it was no use. Her sympathy had been turned back cruelly.

"I see you're still your rotten self—Christmas Eve, or any other night."

"I'm glad you like it."

If there was anything that made her boil quicker than a smart, smug answer. . . .

"I do like it, because it shows me just what kind of a person you really are."

"Temper, temper. . . . "

"Selfish. . . . "

And on they went in petty, futile bickering.

There he was again, she thought, maneuvering himself on the defensive. If they had to have these fights, why wouldn't they have just one where she didn't have to watch all the angles. He didn't argue according to the rules. He always tried to make it look her fault.

"You're so damn spotless," she shouted. "So smug. You couldn't be wrong in a thousand years."

"That's right. Now you're getting smart for a change."

"You're impossible. I don't have to take this from you. I've got plenty of grounds for divorce, if I wanted to use them. I never know where you are at night. You come in at all hours."

"Don't tell your troubles to me. See a lawyer. Don't threaten me with divorce. You know you haven't any grounds that would stand up in court. Try it and see who gives a rat's ass."

"Well, at least you never have to worry about me. You always know where I am."

"The trouble is, I always know. With a lot of damn silly women, shooting off your faces, like cackling hens."

"That's better than racing around with a bunch of other wild stallions."

"Oh, for Christ' sake. Get some clothes on and get the hell out of here. You look ridiculous in nothing but a brassiere and pants."

Connie turned and ran into the bedroom without looking back. Her heart had tightened inside her until she thought it would break. ... She held back the sob that was welling to her throat. Falling prone across the rough spread, she let the tears come silently. She would rather die than let him know that he had hurt her.

Why, why, why? What made them flare at each other like this? Was it their silly pride that made them stand against each other? Refusing to yield that little inch required to form a true partnership.

It hurt so much.

She pressed the spread hard against her mouth so that Ken wouldn't hear the sobs that wracked her throat.

Connie heard the tap running in the bathroom. Ken washing his face and hands. Banging around in the living room, then silence for a long minute, footsteps toward the bedroom door.

Connie ran to lock it, a split second before Ken tried the knob, found it locked, and knocked.

"Open up. Let me in," he said. There was a note of contrition in his voice. "I want to talk to you."

Her tears dried in her eyes. Now was the time to make him pay. She sat up and said nothing. Anger lay deep in her heart.

Ken rattled the door again. The wood creaked as he strained against it with his shoulders.

"C'mon, open up, darling. Let's talk this over."

"There's nothing to talk over. Leave me alone."

"Don't be silly. Open the door."

"No."

"I'm sorry about the mean things I said. Please open the door," he said, urgently.

He could be sugar sweet at times. It was hard to resist him.

"All I want from you is away."

Evidently he gave up, because she could hear him walking back down the hall to the kitchen. Her ears followed his footsteps going across the floor and straight out the back door. In a moment, she heard the engine start, back down the driveway, and grind into low gear. She followed it until it faded into nothing.

Connie rose slowly, stared at herself in the glass. Her thin, dark face was drawn, tiny puffed pouches under her eyes from crying. Her hair was a tangled mess. She patted a dab of powder on her eyes to take away the reddened smudges, then applied a little color. She felt better.

She shuffled around the bedroom listlessly, sliding her feet in Ken's oversize slippers. She wondered what there was about him that made her love him so damn much. Sometimes, he didn't seem to have a heart at all. She had plopped herself on his lap there, in the front room, dressed as daringly as she used to, when they were first married, and he used to get so hot and bothered, he could hardly get her into bed soon enough. But tonight ... he had been so preoccupied with something else, he had hardly noticed her, except for the weight.

She stood in front of the open closet, trying to decide which dress to wear tonight. The black? No. She needed something gay to offset her depression. The black with the tiny strand of pearls at the throat was nice. It gave her a tailored look that she liked, but tonight, a dash of color was needed. She slipped a rust red thing over her sleek hips. It clung tight as moss on a rock, and she enjoyed the sensuous feel of the slinky material shimmering down her thighs.

Ken called it her Campbell dress, because he thought it was just the color of tomato soup. One night, lying together in bed, he told her that if she would give in, he would buy a Cadillac convertible to match it.

Remembering this, her heart filled with a familiar warmth. He was a comfort to have around, when he felt right. But then, she imagined all men were about the same. They had their ups and downs.

As she drew on her hose, she noticed some fine, dark hairs on the calves of her legs. She deplored them momentarily. She fastened the snaps and hitched the seams straight, then slipped her feet into spike heels, because her mood seemed to call for them.

In the other room, she snapped on the radio, fiddling with the knobs, until the set warmed. She tuned in a record show, humming a quick tune along with Kay Starr.

She was listlessly turning the pages of a magazine, glancing at some cartoons, when the doorbell buzzed.

Connie rose uncertainly. Who would it be at this time of night? It was only a quarter of eight, and Gladys had said she wouldn't be able to make it until eight o'clock. In all the time, she had known Gladys, she had never yet been on time. Who was it?

She clicked across the floor, snapped on the porch light, and opened the door.

A blonde girl, holding some sort of package under her arm, blinked behind large glasses at the sudden light. Connie had never seen her before. She must have the wrong house.

"Yes?" Her voice hung in midair.

"You Ken's wife?" the girl asked, looking at her with frank appraisal.

Connie felt like a horse at auction.

"I'm Mrs. Lawrence, if that's what you mean."

"No wonder." The girl kept on staring at her.

"What do you mean?"

"Never mind. You wouldn't understand." She took the box from under her arm. "Take this. It's Ken's."

"How did you happen to get it?"

"Ken was in a hurry and left it in my taxi."

Connie felt herself freezing inside. Several unanswered questions became suddenly clear. No wonder Ken had other things on his mind, but she couldn't honestly say she admired his taste.

There was something cheap about this girl. Her face was garishly made up, her manner of speech, loud and open. It might be prejudice on her part, but Connie doubted it. She wouldn't have liked the girl, if they had met under different circumstances. It was an instinctive personality clash.

Connie took the offered box. She tried a forced smile.

"Won't you come in for a minute? I'm sure Ken would like to thank you when he gets back. He's just gone up town for a minute."

"Thanks—but no, thanks," the girl said. "It wouldn't be much fun to sit and snarl at each other, like a couple of cats, would it? Because that's what we'd do."

"Well, if that's the way you feel. ... "

"It isn't a question of my feelings. It's your natural reaction. The thing to remember is that in this tough world, you've got to give and take. He's not really a bad guy, Mrs. Lawrence. You've just got to humor him. Sometimes, he's like a little kid."

Connie's smile grew a little tighter.

The blonde's eyes widened behind her impossible glasses.

"I see you don't buy that," she said. "Sorry."

She nodded once, and was gone into the darkness. Connie watched her stunned, until she stepped into the waiting cab.

Connie laid the box on the maple side table, gently, and dropped on the couch. The blonde, appearing so suddenly at the door, seemed to fix a huge searchlight in her mind. Its beam coursed the walls of her brain, like a prison guard trapping an escaped prisoner. Disjointed pieces began to fall into place. The nights he had come in late, mostly in the odd hours of the morning, a silly drunken grin on his face, giving her the story that the boys wanted to do a certain thing, and he had gone along for laughs. She had humored him—the blonde would never know how much—and she had believed him beyond endurance.

Because she'd rather die on the spot, than go creeping back to her parents. Broken heart and crushed marriage in her bag. To admit failure at the biggest job she had ever held.

But how far backward can you bend? She knew in her heart, without being told, that Ken had slept with the blonde. That spectacled specimen was no virgin, and she definitely wasn't the type of play for peanuts. And, damn it, neither was Ken.

Maybe that was the trouble. She had humored him, given him the things he wanted, whenever he asked. Had been more mistress to him than wife. But he must be insatiable. One woman was not enough. Secretly, she admitted to herself, that one man was never enough for her. She nearly always hungered, when they had finished. But it was the old double standard. One had to be enough for her.

That damned double standard of morality. A fellow could step out of line as many times as he liked, even if he was married and had sixteen kids at home; and as long as he didn't let his family starve, or lose his head completely, no one would utter a whisper against his fair name. But, just let his wife make eyes at the milkman on the back step, and she would be thrown out of the house in disgrace. What a rotten, doubledealing man's world it was.

But little Connie didn't have to take any more of this. She could leave him flat. Then Ken would be free, just the way he always should have been. His was a gay, soaring spirit that should never have been fettered in marriage.

But how would she live without him?

She dragged into the bedroom in search of cigarettes. She found a crumpled pack in one off Ken's dirty shirts. He always left them in the pocket for her to discover later, broken and shredding, floating on top of the water, after she had thrown the shirt in the washing machine.

The hardest part of the whole thing, she decided, would be the honey sweet smothering she would get from her parents. They would be vindictive against Ken. She couldn't stand that. She knew that some of the misunderstanding between them was her fault. Why should Ken pay for what lay on her head? She hadn't given him her life, her time, and her complete love, since he had been home, and Ken had resented it. If only Mom and Dad could be made to see that some of this was her fault. But she knew their blind, narrow way. Such a thing was impossible.

They would never understand that, in a sense, she had committed adultery too. Not morally or physically, but socially.

What if....

It was such a blinding flash, that it halted the hand that was lighting the cigarette.

What if there was actual proof that she was an adulteress! If she gave Ken the grounds for divorce. Handed it to him on a silver platter. Then, there would be no need to hash out painful details.

Connie elaborated on the idea. Ken would hate her, of course—would be glad to get rid of her. Never remembering the countless nights he had crossed the boundary. She would be a rotten thing, despised by all. But wouldn't it be worth that price to give Ken his freedom, to be rid of her parents? She could go north to San Francisco, or beyond, start all over again.

Her fingers trembled, as she drew the cigarette again to her mouth. Her lips writhed against each other, and in spite of the self-control she struggled to maintain, a tear slipped through on her black eyelash.

God, what an existence. But what else was she to do? Ken had proved he didn't want her, and she wouldn't take charity.

And just this afternoon, she was wishing for a baby. What a laugh. To bring a child into this awful world, to suffer and struggle, and for what? To have your whole life shattered in a few minutes, standing in your own doorway, speaking to a total stranger.

Divorce was never hard on the people that entered into the action, except financially. But for the kids, fastening their tender, developing faith on both the father and mother, it was a bewildering hell.

Connie was glad that she and Ken had never produced.

For the second time that evening, she went into the bathroom, repaired her make-up, gave her ebony hair a last comb, and glanced at the rust gown, approvingly. Noticing the high pride that was apparent in the upward sweep of her breasts, their impudence held firmly in place. She glanced with pleasure at the gentle swell and taper of efficient looking hips. She still had enough of what it takes to get by, she decided.

She ripped a paper towel from a spool that hung by the wash basin and rubbed the lipstick from her mouth. Selecting a brighter shade, she applied it carefully. Then stared at herself in the mirror again. That ought to put her over. She knew that Gladys would be more than happy to substitute a dim, smoky bar for a dull movie, any time. Connie could just imagine what she would say.

"It's about time you wised up."

Maybe. And, again, maybe it was too late.

Could she go through with it?

She went into the kitchen and turned the burner on under the coffee pot. She was just pouring the black liquid into her cup, when she heard the car turn into the drive. She felt herself freezing again. If she could only remain cool. After all, Ken had slammed out of the house. All she had to do was stay on the defensive. It would make the whole thing much easier.

By this time, she thought, he was regretting the whole thing and anxious to make up. Would like everything to be just the way it was before. He would come cringing into the house, like a cur dog, expecting to be thrown out on his tail. He would blurt out something silly, something a small boy would say, and she would have to throttle the instinct to hold him to her breast. She must be strong-willed and not break up at this point.

If she ever let him win her around, she would never be able to go through with her plan.

Connie heard the door open. Now it would start.

He snaked his head around the corner of the breakfast nook, reaching across to tickle the back of her neck. She stiffened.

"Merry Christmas, darling," he said.

That one was so phony, she didn't bother to answer.

"You're not still mad, are you?"

Silence.

"Don't you want to know what I had to eat? Don't you want to know whether or not malnutrition will set in?"

"I'll go along with the gag," she said, letting the cold creep into her voice, so that there would be no mistake how she felt, "what did you have to eat?"

"Hamburger, fries, and a malt." Ken sat across from her. "It was really great. You should've come along."

"You didn't want me there."

"Sure I did. You know I want you with me all the time."

"That's a lie. How can you sit there, lie like that, and be able to look me in the face."

"What do you mean, a lie?"

"Don't bother with any more tricks. I've had my eyes opened tonight. I know you for what you are now."

"What in the great hell are you talking about?" Ken's bewildered eyebrows quivered.

"Just a minute, you sweet, innocent boy, and I'll show you."

Connie rose, stalked into the living room, lifted the box from the table, and in a few minutes, was dressed in the sharkskin suit. As she raged into the kitchen, she was amazed to hear his sigh of relief.

"Good old Beverly." The phrase escaped him involuntarily.

Connie pounced on it.

"So that's her name. She looked like a common bitch. I can't say I admire your taste."

Ken laughed, reaching over to pat her shoulder.

"This is the first time I've seen my baby jealous."

She lashed at him in cold fury. The palm of her hand landed across his cheek with a loud crack. She backed away. Her bottom lip was gripped between her teeth, and she struggled to hold back the tears. Her voice quavered when she spoke.

"Get your hands off me. If you need a woman, go back to your Beverly. She'll take care of you. Or one of the other floozies that the dear, sweet boys force you into picking up. I don't want any part of you. And the quicker you get it through that conceited head, the better off we'll both be."

She saw the muscles in his cheeks stiffen, as he gritted his teeth in a sudden, wild rage. He raised his fist and came at her, slowly stopping, as his anger cooled with the deflation of his ego. All the air seemed to go out of him, as though he were a penny balloon that had met disaster from the point of a pin. He turned slowly, and left the room.

Connie had never intended to carry the argument so far. If she meant her plan to work, it would never do to face him with his own moral crimes. She would have to make him think the fault lay on her side. Impossible as it sounded, she would have to line her own parents against her, on Ken's side.

What a hell of a life it was, when everything you did or said, had to be on one side of the fence, or the other, and before you did anything, you had to consider every angle.

She was sitting on the couch, smoking a cigarette, when she heard Ken come out of the bedroom, and rummage in the coffee can on the top shelf, where they kept their spare change. It was her household money, and any other time she would have argued bitterly, before she let him take a nickel of it; but now, nothing seemed to matter. Let him blow it all. What was the difference? The inner strength that had kept her going, had melted away. There had been other times when doubts and fears had crowded in on her, but she had cast them all aside. Now she knew the truth. Their marriage had been a farce from the beginning. Let him throw the money away. From now on, he would be alone.

After tonight, he'd want to spit in her face.

She sat on the couch quietly, listening to Ken stomp around the bedroom in frustrated rage, a lump in her throat like a knotted fist, when Gladys rang the doorbell. Twenty minutes late.

8:30 P.M.

A FEVER of rage mounted in him, flaming so intensely as to make him grind his teeth until they ached. Then dying away to the tiniest whisper in ever diminishing crescendos. It was nothing more than a momentary flash that was soon gone, leaving him to think clearly again.

No matter how it hurt his pride, Ken could clearly see that Connie had been right. After all, he had shacked with the blonde. But could anyone foresee a quirk of fate like this? The damn woman you spend the afternoon with in bed, turning up at the house. Meeting your wife. It was one of those things that you heard of happening to someone else, and you always got a large yak out of the other guy's troubles.

But this time, it had happened to him. Of course, he couldn't be sure of what Beverly had said, but he doubted that she had spilled everything. It wasn't normal for a woman to spread the inside story of her lover's intimate techniques to said lover's wife. Who probably knew more of them than she.

But you couldn't tell about Bev. Not that damn psycho.

One thing in her favor; she had returned the suit. He'd have to give her credit for that. Not that it was a Christmas present any more, with Connie wearing it. He was in the doghouse, but good.

Connie had really given him the word. She was such a passive girl, when it came to any kind of trouble, that he had forgotten just how fiery she could get.

Don't kid yourself, Pal. You're not going to kick that kid around for very long, before you get it back with interest. And right in the teeth.

Ken sat on the bed and was slipping off his shoes, when he heard the bell ring. A pair of heels clicked across the floor, and after some high chipping laughter with someone at the door, brought another pair back with them. It was that crazy Gladys. What a meathead. She would probably be just right for Connie tonight. Cheer her up. Do her good.

Connie slipped silently in the door. Her face was frozen tight, and after one hopeful glance, Ken turned his attention to his shoes and kept it riveted there, until she had gotten her light coat out of the closet and gone back into the living room.

Ken's spirits were in the sewer. She was madder than hell. He couldn't remember seeing her as sore as she was right now. But she had never caught him in this kind of thing before. He had always said there'd be hell to pay, if she ever found out. Well, she had.

The front door slammed, forming an exclamation point to his thoughts. In a few seconds, he heard Gladys' engine roar. She rode the clutch too much. Most women did. He formed a mock salute.

Good luck, Connie, my sweet. See you never.

He stripped to his shorts, stepping into the bathroom. He turned on the shower, waiting for the water to warm a little, before he stepped in. The sharp needles dug at his back, but it was great. He let his mind drift as the water grew warmer, running through the hair on his legs. Even the glutting gurgle of the rushing stream, making its exit through the drain, was something to take his mind away from the crisis that confronted him. He welcomed it.

He soaped various portions of his body vigorously, allowing the tingling deluge to rinse him immediately. He was low in the mind, but here was a simple, sensuous exhilaration that he could take pleasure in, without thinking too much. He made the most of it.

Stepping out on the mat, he reached in, shutting off the water. Rivulets dripped from his tawny skin to the linoleum floor, making tiny, wet craters where they fell. Ken's skin had retained most of the golden tan he had gotten on the beach last summer. He had spent the majority of his week ends in an old pair of trunks, when the fickle California sun allowed it.

He glanced into the mirror over the wash basin. It was clouded by steam from the shower. He gave it a swipe with his damp towel, wiping away the moisture, grimacing at his reflection.

He was thirty years of age, and the mirror showed him he looked every year of it tonight. He ran some hot water into the bowl and started to lather his face. The razor soothed him, as it slid over the stubble, like a jack plane over a pine board.

He hadn't admitted it to himself yet, but his subconscious knew what was in store for him. He would take some dough that he knew Connie had stashed away, and he would go out on a solo binge. Was there a nicer way to celebrate Christmas, he thought grimly.

Back in the bedroom, he dressed, concentrating on the details of getting his clothes on, keeping his mind a blank forcibly.

But, in spite of his rigid barriers, his thoughts kept rolling back to Connie. She was meek, and had never raised a fuss with him before. With a definite personality, of course, but never one that intruded itself upon your own. Little by little, slow as time, insidious as malaria, she came to possess you. You were her captive. If by nothing else, her charm of spirit.

He sat on the bed, staring dully at the closet door. Everything in this room was tied inseparably to her. How could you look at anything in it, without having a vison of her lovely, slender, curving form in front of your eyes.

He pounded the pillow at his side, thinking of the nights they had spent in this room. Ken shook his head slightly, as though to clear it. He was practiced at setting Connie aside, into her little cubbyhole, but tonight, she wouldn't stay put. Even as he rummaged through the various places Connie hid her house money, she kept peeking out at him, reproaching him. He couldn't seem to shake her.

But he was in luck. He found twenty dollars in an old fruit jar, at the back of the top dresser drawer. Under a pile of crumpled silk stockings. Quickly, he tucked it in his pocket, together with the change he had taken from the kitchen, and, snapping off the lights, locked the door, as he left.

The car sounded like the greeting of an old friend, as he tramped on the starter. He rammed the tiny car up the street to the nearest intersection. He made a right turn, slowed his speed, cruising slowly in the curb lane. There wasn't any sense in hurrying, if you weren't sure where you were going.

He didn't feel like seeing any of the guys. They'd be sure to ask him how come he was out on Christmas Eve. Where was his old lady? He could imagine the ribbing he'd take, if he told them the actual truth.

No, it wouldn't do to go to any of his regular hangouts. There was a good chance that some of the guys would show. He just didn't feel like seeing anyone he knew.

Maybe he ought to head east. Outside of town. There were a lot of little joints out there that looked real honky-tonky—rough, tough, where your safest spot was with your back to the wall, with a bottle in your hand. They were outside the city limits, in county territory, where the little law they had came around very seldom. They were outside the city police jurisdiction, and only the sheriff's office, or the state cops gave them a going over, one in a while.

He had heard about them, had wondered, and tonight, he was in the mood for a little exploration. Any place that was new.

It wouldn't do to saunter into one of these joints, all duded up. Some touchy joker might peg you for a plain clothes operator.

Not that anybody was on the jump from the law, they just liked it cagey. Most everyone that came into these little places on the east side of town, was from Oklahoma, East Texas and around. Remnants of the Dust Bowl migration that had paraded families west in '36. They had been kicked around, beaten, robbed, forced into slavery, before the war. Now that they had attained independence through a living wage at defense plants and other factories, they had grouped themselves in tiny settlements all over the state, to form a strength of numbers against the bigoted world, ringed against them. Clannish as Scots, they had certain customs, and an intricate dialect that differed from the accepted standard.

They were more distant with strangers than the proverbial Vermont flat land farmer. The aftermath of "The Grapes of Wrath."

Ken removed his tie with one hand, as he stopped at a light. He threw it into the glove compartment, as he unbuttoned his collar. Now he would be dressed in the current fashion. Except for the fact that he wore a suit. Most of the rubes would be in Levis and T-shirts. He felt much as Columbus must have, as he set sail from the Canary Islands, the last known landfall.

As Ken glanced up at the neon lights streaming by the window, he noticed a replica of an old wagon wheel, outlined in the fluorescent tubing, extending from a windowed front. Back of the glass, the usual neon beer ads hung, beckoning. Making his signal, Ken swerved in to the curb.

He could feel the atmosphere of the tiny place, before he sat down on one of the stools that lined the bar. That of an old country tavern that has been by the side of the main pike for centuries, receiving any passengers that might stop for a bite of quick food and a mug of stout. It seemed almost medieval to Ken, for a moment. He noticed that the bartender obviously didn't welcome any new trade, but catered to the same handful of regulars that came in every night.

Four of them were playing knock poker at the upper end of the bar. The bartender, laying down his hand, with obvious reluctance, waddled down, to stand truculently in front of Ken.

Ken glanced around to see what the others were drinking.

"Draw me one," he said.

The bartender nodded, without a word, held a sparkling glass under the tap, lifting it to measure the head. Scraping the foam with a flat, polished stick of ivory, he slid the glass forward.

"What's the fare?" Ken fished for his wallet.

"Fifteen."

In less than a minute, the bartender had shoveled his change out on the bar, and was back up at the other end of the counter, staring concentratedly at his cards.

Ken sipped at the cold beer, tasting a bit rancid to his mouth that had had so much bourbon tipped into it that afternoon. He looked around him again. He was a stranger. He felt their eyes flicking over him, and having measured him, they no longer knew he was there. Sitting like so many geese, gabbling, cackling, laughing at each other, and he wasn't a part of any of it. A couple of guys were staring moodily into their glasses. Well, they could keep this joint, for all he cared. It wasn't any bargain anyway.

Two long shuffleboards, their polished hardwood gleaming in the bright light, ran parallel down the center of the room. Sprinkled with powdery wax, chrome buttons resting idly.

Damn, what a hole. He was goddamned bored.

Ken drifted back to a garishly lit juke box. By diligently searching through all the pieces listed, he found one he liked. Something by Louis Jordan. The rest were Westerns. He punched a nickel in the slot and stood a moment, watching the smooth operation of the mechanism behind the thick glass.

"John, why'n hell don't you smash that record?" One of the card sharks said for Ken's benefit, as he walked back to his stool. "Ever' time some dude comes in off the street, that's the bastard that comes up."

"There's no accountin' for taste, Ed."

He burned. Gripped his hand tight around his glass. No use to blow up in this cracker box. Too many of them. They didn't like him anyway. They'd never seen him before, therefore he was someone to be suspected. Ken couldn't imagine what they'd suspect him of, but there it was. Like a bunch of damn mountain goats, looking down from the rocks.

He ordered another beer and crossed to one of the shuffleboards. He wouldn't let a bunch of rubes beat him out, by God. He tilted the glass to his mouth and let the beer run in. The second glass tasted better; his mouth was getting used to the stuff. Setting the beer on the table, next to the shuffleboard, he grasped one of the pucks uncertainly. He noted the lines drawn at each end of the board, and the numbers. Evidently, the object was to slide the puck from one end of the board to the other, getting the thing close to the end, without actually sliding off into the trough.

"Dime a game," the bartender shouted at him. Ken waved his hand.

The first one he tried was a failure. The board was slick as glass, and the metal disc cannoned off the far end. The next one was as bad. In an effort to get the range, his throw was weak, and this time, the puck stopped in the middle.

It was intriguing. He had often wondered what the game was like. He tried several more times, before he could get it close to the end. He was feeling proud of himself, because he hung one over the edge, down at the far corner, and turned away for another sip of beer. When he turned back, there was someone else at the board, sighting the length of it, slowly sliding a puck up and down the outside edge. When he let it go, the iron button arced slowly across the width of the board, barely nudging off the disc that Ken was so proud of, and took its place.

Ken's eyes widened over his glass.

"And that's how you play shuffleboard," the ace said, straightening up from the board.

"Yes, I guess," Ken said, looking the stranger over.

Probably the ugliest man Ken could ever remember seeing. His entire appearance was symbolized by a great, dirty, parrot beak of a nose. Covered with blackheads, broken, canted down one side of his seamed face, it was the point where one's attention was immediately focused. Only later, did you take in the tiny pig eyes, set close together, and the thin gash, that was his mouth. The lips were never quite closed, and you caught a hint of brown, sharp teeth.

There was no neck, and the head ran directly into a pair of brutish arms and shoulders that seemed ready to burst the bounds of the flimsy shirt he wore. His hands were in proportion to the rest of his huge body. Lumpy knuckles covered with a dark growth, that might have been hair, and the gnarled fingers were capped with broken nails. A pair of greasy jeans looked out of place with the flaming red sport shirt he wore. His shirt was the only reputable piece of clothing on him. His feet, like a pair of snow shovels, were encased in massive pair of motorcycle boots, from which the buckles were long since missing.

He hadn't noticed Ken's scrutiny, because as soon as he had finished his modest statement, he turned to the board again and proceeded to remove and replace the puck that he had left there, in place of Ken's.

"You must play quite a bit," Ken said.

"You kiddin'? I live on a damned shuffleboard. It's easy to see you never played before."

"I guess it is. I'm lousy."

"You're tellin' me. But, hell, everyone is when they start. It's like anything else. Takes practice."

"How about showing me a few shots?"

"It'll cost."

"I'm a pigeon. What's the price?"

"Easy. Loser pays for the game and the beer."

"Fair enough."

It was a cinch that the man in the vivid shirt was no novice. He cuddled the pucks lovingly in his large hands, gently coasting them the length of the board, to rest defiantly on the outermost section. When Ken would place one, accidentally, in scoring position, the big man's massive left arm would shoot a metal disc out with vengeance, and like the crack of a whip, the puck would snap Ken's marker from the board.

Score of the first game was 21 to 8.

"What'll you have?" Ken asked.

"I'm not gonna bleed you yet. Just a glass."

"Draw two," Ken yelled at the bartender.

"You know, fella, you could really play this game, if you wanted to."

"What do you mean?"

"Well, when you shove the puck, you gotta give it a little hook. Just like in bowling. You ever bowl any?"

"Sure."

"Well, you know you always get more control on a hook, than trying to roll a straight ball. Well, it's the same way with shuffleboard. Let's try it again, and I'll show you what I mean."

"I'm game. Shoot."

"I ain't goin' to bleed you for no beer, this time. Each guy pays his own way. I thought you was a sharpie lookin' for a sucker to milk, before. But after watchin' you play a game, I can see you aren't. Let's see. I was the winner, so I go first."

Ken lost two quick games in succession. He began to get the feel of the thing. A certain heft to your throw, correctly gauging the length of the board, and you can get it down into a reasonable scoring position. How a player was able to place one of the elusive little markers in any position on the board, maintain perfect control of the damn little things, was more than he knew, at this stage of his training. He doubted that he would ever know, but the fact that the evidently clumsy, ignorant man, next to him, was such a master at the game, presented a kind of challenge to him. He had to find the secret. Also, and not least, in his mind, was the fact that Connie was out tonight, so mad at him, that everything they had ever known together, might be on the rocks for good. Shuffleboard was as good a way as any to forget. For a little while anyway.

The big man tapped him on the shoulder.

"My turn to buy you one."

"Okay, I'll have the same."

"Another game?"

"Why not?"

"Do you know we've been talking here for twenty minutes, and I don't even know your name?"

"Ken Lawrence."

"Well, all my friends just call me Mizoo. None of 'em dare call me by my right name. Mizoo's easier to remember, 'cause that's where I come from. Near Bloomfield, Missouri."

"I was born here. In Pasadena."

"Damn. You're a rare bird. A native. I thought the Okies and Arkies had taken over this state."

"Not all of it. But damn near."

"Believe me, Pal, they have this part."

"Yeah, I know. How about around here? There any live joints? Any action?"

"Depends on what you're lookin' for. Gamblin'? Babes?"

"I don't give a rat's ass. Anything for a little fun. What are you out for?"

"A little nooky, if it's easy to come by. I can always stir up a little excitement. Whyn't you come with me?"

"Where you going?"

"Honky-tonkin'. All over. Just cruisin'. I know all these joints. Been livin' in 'em, since I got out of the dogfaces."

"What do you do to pay expenses?"

"Swamp on a truck some. Belong to the Sunshine club, mostly."

FRED MALLOY

"Sunshine club?"

"Unemployment insurance. 52-20. Lots of us professional civilian soldiers do. We're just waitin' for another war to come along, so we can pay the government back."

"Oh. How come you work part time on a truck?"

"That ain't very often. That's so I won't look like a plain bum to the Veteran's Administration bitch that gives me my check. She's always askin' whether I worked in the last week, and I think it kinda makes the old girl feel happy when I've picked up a couple bucks."

"That figures."

"Well, let's ramble. I know livelier joints than this. If you want women, I know plenty around this part of town. I'll fix you up."

"I don't give a damn. If they're there, we might as well give them a play."

"You might as well know right now, I'm just about flat," Mizoo said, taking his wallet out and opening it, so Ken could see the contents. "Three dollars and eighty-seven cents, between me and next Monday's relief check. Still want to go? You may have to buy me some more beer."

"I had a twenty-dollar bill when I walked in. We can go until that's gone."

"Then let's hit the trail, sport. We'll keep track of the beer you pay for, and we'll consider it a loan. I'll pay you back as soon as I get my check."

A sense of excitement filled Ken as he followed the big man outside. As ugly as a warped fence, dried and stained by the elements, there was something compelling about Mizoo. He was brash, loud, and apparently didn't any more care what he said than the clouds cared where they rained. He shambled like a bear, and Ken pondered the impossibility of besting him, in a free-for-all. It would be murder to go against him. There was a tiny doubt lurking in the back of Ken's mind as to whether Mizoo was being chummy or was interested in beer and a certain twenty-dollar bill.

"You got a car here, I hope?" Mizoo asked.

"Sure. You?"

"Nah. My old woman's got it. Gone over to her ma's place. I let her have it right in the nose, the bitch."

"Your wife giving you trouble, too?"

"Nothin' else. You?"

"Jesus, yes."

"What's your trouble, Pal?"

"Nothing much. The girl I was laying with, showed up at the house to talk things over with my wife, that's all."

Mizoo croaked with laughter.

"Honest to God? Holy jumped up Jesus, what a spot! And I thought I had miseries."

They had walked up the sidewalk to Ken's Ford. Mizoo opened the door on the right side, slipping into the seat. He lit a cigarette and said, "Oh, what the hell, Ken, boy. It's all over now. It's slop for the hogs. You're in the soup now, you might as well make the most of it. Have fun tonight; tomorrow your wife might have you in the city jail."

"That the way you look at it?"

"Sure. My old lady and I, we're always into it, having a free-for-all. I tell her to stick it. What the hell. I go out when I damn well please, and so does she. I don't give a damn where she goes, or when."

"But damn it, Mizoo. You can't afford a divorce in this state."

"My old lady's Catholic. She ain't goin' through no divorce."

"Wish I could say that."

"Hell, I'm not happy about it. I wish she would clear out. I get sick of seein' her around. You're better off when you don't have no damn woman around to worry about. I wish to hell I'd never seen her. Nothin' but trouble."

"I don't feel that way. I just wish that today hadn't happened."

Why don't you wise up, Ken? Think of all the babes there are in this world that you haven't slept with yet. How are you going to make them happy, when you're tied down at home?"

"Don't bring that up. I can't even keep the ones happy that I've got, without worrying about the millions that I'll probably never meet."

"Well, anyway, it's a pleasant thought. You got to admit that," Mizoo said. Then, after a moment's meditation. "Well, what are we doin'? Let's get this show on the road. Get this crate movin'. Let's meet a few of those unknown babes right now."

At Mizoo's direction, Ken headed further east, the road straight as a plumb line, with high magnesium street lamps threading the length of it, as far as he could see. It was a clear night, with the air as thick and heavy as satin. You could almost feel the texture of it.

Ken wondered what Connie was doing. How was he ever going to square this mess with her. Or should he? She seemed eager enough to flounce out of the house, her pride held high for everyone to see. Or was it pride? There had been several times, lately, more than he liked to think about, when she had been cold and distant towards him. He hated to think such a thing, but it could just be possible that she was interested in someone else. That she didn't really care if he was out catting around, because it gave her a legitimate excuse to be doing the same thing. No, not Connie. She wasn't that kind of a girl. She was honest, which was more than Ken could honestly say for himself. If she was fooling around, she would have had a showdown and called quits with him, before.

Then, what kind of a rat does that make you, a silent voice asked. Just a complete, Grade A crumb, that's all. This long, tall, brunette with a shape that would make some of the professional beauties look like Neantherdal cave women. You've really thrown it out the window this time, you silly bastard. What's happened since you got out of O.D.'s? You've lied to that girl, cheated on her, stole her money, and still, she went on loving you. Why don't you do the right thing for once in your rotten life?"

But what is the right thing, he asked himself.

Maybe she had chances, with her face and figure, to go out with guys that had dough, while you were gone. Real dough. Maybe she went, how do you know?

If she did, I don't want to know about it.

Let's say that she did have opportunities to go out and have some times with guys that don't have to work for any damn insurance company for their bread and butter. Connie isn't the kind that would rat on a guy while he was away. No more than she could now.

But how about you? How about that little babe in Liege? The night you went out in the snow, in her backyard to chop wood with nothing but an overcoat thrown over your shorts?

And that German fraulein in Bad Oberdorf, who gave her father one pack of cigarettes out of the carton you had just given her, to stay downstairs to keep the fire going, while she was in bed with you.

Face it. The best thing you can do is give Connie an easy way out. Let her get a divorce. She'll be happier in the long run. Let her live the good life with someone that really appreciates her. It isn't too late for her. She's only twenty-seven years of age, and she's beautiful, lovely; there's lots of guys that would want her, and she hasn't been ruined by having kids.

That was another thing. She'd always wanted a baby. Maybe he was the one that was sterile, that was all shot. He'd read in some medical book once, that it was usually the fault of the husband in childless marriages. Maybe if he quietly stepped out of the picture, Connie could snag a man that was really a man, and beget a litter of kids.

He could picture himself, sometime in the future, coming back to the old place on Hidalgo Street, some strange guy out front, watering a lawn that had once been his, and then passing

him without a word, just going up to the front door in easy familiarity, showing that he knew the place, when it was painted a lime
green, and not the awful shade of blue that it was now, ringing
the doorbell, standing back a foot from the door, tense. And the
door would open, and in a moment of stunning surprise, there
would be Connie, with a baby on her arm, and one hanging on
her apron, and she might be a little older, with a few crow's feet,
the smile of life around her eyes, but she would still be the same
as far as he was concerned, breathtakingly beautiful. A distant,
dark beauty, as rare and unattainable as the native Eidelweiss,
sparkling from the crags of the Swiss Alps. There would be a half
smile on her face, for just a second, his face half forgotten by the
drifting snows of time, her mind clicking back over the years,
but then, after she had recognized him, she would invite him
into the house out of pity, and a sense of shame at having her
past life parade in front of her children. He would note with envy
their proud new furniture, at the obvious health of the entire
little group, and for a few moments they would struggle to recap-
ture some little memory of their old life together, some common meeting ground for the halting conversation, but whatever
moments they had shared were gone from her, and it was plain to
see that too many things had come between for her to feel anything from them, though they had always been poignantly alive
for him, and after a few feeble efforts, the conversation would
die into an awkward silence. Then the husband would come in,
sit heavily in a chair that was clearly his, by virtue of its having
been placed beside an upright ash tray, with that air of owning
everything within range of vision. They would urge him to stay
for supper, with a certain lack of depth to their invitation, and
he would accept the cue and leave gracefully, quietly, with tears
flooding his heart. A ship that passed in the night.

Mizoo broke into his revery.

"Middle of the next block's the place."

"Right."

Ken was glad of the interruption to his thoughts. God, what a morbid trend he had been following. Was he ever feeling sorry for poor little Ken Lawrence? What the hell, even though he had decided to split with Connie for her own good, it wasn't necessarily the end of the world. He'd still be alive, and as Mizoo had said, there were plenty of women he hadn't met yet.

Tonight, he'd howl. One cause for divorce coming up.

"Okay, pull 'er in here," Mizoo directed. "This ought to be a fairly live joint. Let's case the place, see if we can bootleg some stray quiff out of here."

Every one of these places looked the same, out at this end of town, Ken decided. Little and dirty, looking like nothing more than shoeboxes set down in the midst of vacant lots. Crummy, squalid, with a seamy life of their own, the stale aroma of beer seeming to seep from their walls. But, on the other hand, they were more of a social center, than a place to spend huge sums of money, like the ebony and chrome bourbon bon-tons downtown. People around this part of town had fierce loyalty for their own beer joints; whiskey was never sold as these places weren't licensed for it. Each neighborhood had its own hangout and bowling leagues and softball teams were organized out of each honky-tonk, the patrons of one engaging the regulars of another, in any kind of sport.

As he held the door for Mizoo, the smoke and crashing rag piano hit him in the face with stunning concussion. A vast blur of sound seemed to leap at him from the tables and the minute dance floor. Women giggling, men shouting across the floor from the booths that lined the wall, to the long bar that extended the length of the room. Down at the far end, away from the door, under a large electric clock, seated at an unbelievably scarred and Worn piano, with the face gone, so you could see the hammers pounding on the cords, sat possibly the strangest member of the crowd. Under a saucy, felt lady's hat, with veil, flowers and all the trimmings, sat the piano player in his shirt sleeves. He was in his sixties, bouncing to the beat of the ragtime he was pounding out with savage strokes on the aged instrument, beating the piano so hard with each bass chord, that it was a miracle the thing didn't collapse into a stack of kindling. The old man never looked at the keys, but turned his head continually from side to side, chatting with people he knew, shouting in a high shrill voice, over the roaring noise of the crowd. Occasionally, he would turn his head toward the microphone that stood at his side, and sing some obscene verse that he had apparently just thought up.

Ken and Mizoo pushed their way toward the bar. They were jostled and shoved by the dancing, jumping horde, as they tried to cross the dance floor. Mizoo usually gave the offenders such a push in return, that they almost lost their balance. One glance at his bulk, usually drove any thought of revenge from their minds.

"What are you going to have this time?" Ken asked, when they had gained the comparative security of the bar.

"Don't matter what you want. You gotta figure what's best to impress the babes."

"How can you make any impression with beer?"

"Simple. In here, we buy beer by the quart. That shows any gal that might be interested, that we don't care a damn about our buck. We're easy spenders. We can also pour them a little out of our bottle, without running too short."

"Very smart. And we won't have to be running through that mob on the floor, every couple minutes."

"Now you're beginning to think a little."

They got a quart apiece from the bartender, who was leaning against the large mirror that faced the bar, figuring on a racing form.

"Your powers of concentration are great," Ken said. "How can you figure races with all this going on?"

"Them actors?" The bartender sighed. "They don't bother me none. Hell, when you hear 'em all the time, like me, you don't hear 'em no more."

Ken shrugged his shoulders, as he and Mizoo turned from the bar, attempting a perilous return to the opposite side of the squirming, jumping mass of humanity.

Mizoo nudged him with an elbow. Several couples were embracing fiercely in the booths. One of the couples released his partner, long enough to glare at them. Mizoo led on with obvious indifference.

Again, they stared at one couple surrendering their passion in a kiss, straining to possess one another as much as they could in a crowded, lighted room. The man's hand roamed at will, inside her blouse, looking like tiny moving rodents under the diaphanous material. It was obvious the girl's moral reserve was dwindling fast. She lay on her side, as much as possible, in the tiny booth, her hands locked around the back of her partner, one leg around his, six inches of white velvet flesh showing above her stocking top, beneath the hem of her raised skirt. Her hair was tumbled in disarray about her face, and her dark lidded eyes were lightly closed in straining emotion.

Mizoo and Ken watched the frustrated gyrations, for nearly five minutes, before the male protagonist sensed that possibly all things were not right in his world. Slowly, he broke from the locked embrace of the girl and turned, facing his audience.

"What in hell's ailin' you bastards? Seen enough?"

Ken was inclined to sympathize with the man in his anger.

"Don't mind us, Jack. We're just window shopping."

"Well, move on, Slim. This ain't no show we're puttin' on."

Mizoo didn't share Ken's tolerant view of the situation. He moved up on a level with Ken, taking a nonchalant sip from his glass of beer.

"What's bitin' you, fella? 'Fraid we're going to horn in on your piece?"

"I'm not afraid of a goddam thing," the man said, rising to his feet, his girl coming into a state approaching normalcy, stared around her in wonder. "How about you?"

"Not a thing in the world, chum," Mizoo exhaled a steady stream of smoke in the other fellow's face.

If neither of them were afraid, Ken had his doubts. The man they were facing stood a good six feet tall, almost level with Ken, and he was of a solid huskiness that foreboded strength and persistence in battle.

"There's only one way to prove that to me, you yellow son-of-a-bitch," the man said. "Choose me to go outside and settle up."

"Settle up for what, Bastard. We ain't done nothin' that needs settlin'." Mizoo's voice fairly purred.

"I'm saying you did, and if you're arguin' with me, it's the same as callin' me a liar. And I don't like to be called a liar."

"There's not much you do like, is there, Bastard?"

The big man moved in on Mizoo and made a quick grab at his shirt front, but Mizoo's right arm, as heavy and as hard as a log of oak, chopped his opponent's arm away, before it could get a grip.

"Don't touch that shirt, Bastard, it's pretty," Mizoo said.

"I won't touch it, you son-of-a-bitch, I'll rip it right off your back."

"I don't think so. I don't think you're quite enough man for the job."

The girl had been squirming her clothing into shape, struggling to get out of the booth and over to where the three of them stood. She pulled at her man's sleeve.

"Come on now, Mike. Let's not have any trouble in this place. Leave these fellows alone. Let's go some place else. I'm sure they didn't mean anything by what they were doing."

The man shook her off his arm.

"Like hell they didn't. They're as bad as peeping Toms. I'll close their goddamn eyes with my fists."

"I wanted you to quit in this public place. I told you there were too many people around," she whined.

"Oh, lay off. That ain't the point. These bastards got it coming to them, and I'm the boy to do the job. They're too damn smart. Now shut up, and sit down."

The girl melted back into the booth. Mizoo dropped his cigarette to the floor, ready for anything that might happen.

"Now that you got your woman straightened out, what are you going to do about us?" Mizoo smiled gently. "We may not be tough, but there's two of us."

"I don't give a damn if there's eight. I got to go to the can. I'll see you bastards out in back."

Mizoo gave him a mock salute, and turned, smiling at the frightened girl that sat rigidly watching the departing back of her boy friend.

"Don't mind if we set our beer here while we take care of a little unfinished business, do you? We'll be back for it, and we promise you we won't be too hard on him."

She glanced up at them as they placed their quart bottles and half-filled glasses on the table.

"It's not him that I'm worried about."

"Cut it out, lady. You're scarin' me to death."

Down the room behind the piano, through a door, stood two doors at right angles to each other. One led to the Men's and the other, outside. Mizoo, seeming familiar in his surroundings, led the way down the side and around to a little cleared area in back. It was a natural place for a fight. It had probably been laid out for just this purpose. It abutted a narrow alley, along which were parked two cars, shielding it from outside view, and running lengthwise away from them, down the length of the building, was an eight-foot cypress hedge. Forming the other two sides of the square, the wooden frame building, in the shape of an "L," was lined with barrels, filled with empty bottles and cans. They cut off the light from the street, making the gloom of the arena almost impenetrable.

Ken shifted from one foot to the other, lighting one cigarette from the stub of another, tense with anticipation.

"What's holding our friend up? Why doesn't he show up?"

"Scared?"

"Hell, no. I just want to know when he's going to make his play, that's all."

"I know that guy. I've heard about how he works. He won't show up here until he's got a couple of buddies with him. You don't think a guy's going to deliberately step into two to one odds, do you?"

Before Ken could frame a reply, their opponent, striding slowly and quietly, was upon them. Ken couldn't have spoken, because in that instant, a heavy hand grasped his shoulder, spinning him around, filled his mouth with hard, charging knuckles, and down he went, sprawling in the loose dirt.

"You're the one I choose first," the heavy man said, snarling. "You're my first patsy."

"It's your party. Go ahead," Mizoo said, smiling.

Ken, momentarily dazed by the surprise blow, stared in wonder at Mizoo. His friend was throwing him to the wolves. He wasn't going to do a damn thing, but stand there and let this big ape eat him up. Goddamn if he could do that. He'd get up and kill this guy, rip and tear him to pieces, by God, dirty, kick him in the nuts, anything, just to nail him, and then, by God, if he could still stand on his feet and catch a breath, he'd finish Mizoo too. What a cheap, lousy trick. Start a fight, choose a guy outside, and then let your buddy take over.

He started slowly drawing his feet under him, hoping he wouldn't be seen by his deadly enemy, before his eyes became adjusted to the dark. That was his advantage, the only one he had. The guy he was fighting was just as tall as he was, had a longer reach, and had him by twenty pounds in weight. If he could only jump the guy while he was beating his brains out at Mizoo, while the ape thought he was stunned.

The legs seemed to want to rush under him, and it was hard to take it easy. Finally, they were there. The muscles in his calves were like cords, taut and tight. He raised himself to his hands, and launched himself.

It was good when he felt the impact of his raging fist on that hated soft belly. It gave with a whoosh, and the man staggered three or four paces, before he caught his balance. A roundhouse left whistled not an inch before Ken's face, but he was expecting it and rolled before it came.

He got his guard up and deflected the following right cross, but he felt the power behind the blow. The guy's a monster, he thought. All he had to do was tag Ken once, and the party would be over.

A looping right caught Ken high on the cheek, snapping him cruelly out of his revery. Ken knew what to do, how to figure him now, and he couldn't do it worrying about anything but the immediate problem.

He waited for the next fast arcing left hand and ducked it easily, countering with an upsurging right hand that crashed on the point of the man's jaw. His opponent was stunned for a flash second, reeling back against the frame building, spilling a barrel of beer cans and a couple of wine bottles. They went cascading, rolling with tiny prisms of reflections winking in the faraway light from the street.

Ken felt icy as he waited a split second, deciding how to follow this new advantage. He jumped at his opponent, but the man was waiting. A foot ripped out, catching him with rib crushing force in the pit of the stomach, and tiny, sparkling lights swam before his eyes, and he went sagging to his knees in the dirt, wanting to puke, scrabbling at the rim of one of the barrels. He felt numb from the waist down. He could see the guy coming at him, but he couldn't do anything to stop him.

A fist blasted him across the mouth, and it seemed the inside of his cheek was ripped, and his teeth creaked in their sockets, and then the dazzling impact came again from the other side, and his head rocked. A hand reached down, grabbing him by the slack lapels of his coat, jerking him upward, but he was still an empty, rasping husk, with not a breath of wind inside him, but the big fellow kept pounding him, and where was Mizoo? He was probably getting a charge out of watching a damn-yankee take a deserved beating. Well, goddammit, he had a message for Mr. Mizoo. He wasn't going to be cleaned. Even if he got killed, he was going to get some lumps in.

His new fury tapped strength from some unsuspected new reservoir. His knee came surging up, a wild, uncontrolled action, pounding into his enemy's groin, the kneecap tearing into the vulnerable spot.

The big fellow screamed and fell away from him into the dirt, huddled, writhing, on the ground, and in his pain, cursing at the top of his lungs. Ken stooped to reach for the front of his shirt, to lash out, crush and maim his face with repeated straight lefts, grinding and smashing, until his arm was numb to the elbow. Snarling, he leaned over, his fist ready for the kill, but he never made it.

For the second time in the space of seconds, someone grabbed his coat, ripping it this time. He was spun around and got a straight left hand to the mouth. Ken staggered back, tripped on the huddled form of his former enemy, and went down on his back. When the haze cleared, he could see that three of them stood crouched, a few yards away. It was plain that they had waited until their leader was on the ground, before rushing Ken. Now they were waiting to finish him, fix him good, and leave him in the alley.

In a startled second, he saw and understood why Mizoo had stood back, waiting. He had figured on just such a trick as this. Ken could see the stocky silhouette, bent so low, that his walk was like a crawl, picking up speed now, rushing with a growl and a yell, like some jungle animal, full tilt into the middle of the three men.

Before Mizoo could reach them, however, the one that had looped the left hand at Ken's jaw, leaped, feet first, at his prostrate form.

Ken was waiting. As the 'cycle boots came flying toward him, he reached out quickly, grasping and twisting. The direction of the leap deflected, the force gone, his opponent went down in the dirt beside him. Ken scrambled up. He blasted the face of the man who had tried to jump him, again and again. The nose on the hated face gushed blood, as though it were a fountain, and the head sagged from inside like a sack full of suet on a string.

But the will to live is strong.

A pair of strong hands reached out, winding around Ken's legs. A quick snatch, using maybe the last ounce of strength in his possession, and the opponent had Ken on his back again. Ken could just barely discern the bloody mask getting set to go after him again. But the man was too far gone to jump, and fumbling inside his shirt, he produced a knife, glittering and cold.

Ken rolled out of the man's reach, and was on his feet in an instant. He aimed a vicious kick at his enemy, and the man went down again. He twitched once and was still.

His chest heaving, struggling to get air in his lungs, Ken stood staring at Mizoo, swearing at the top of his voice, as he punched at his two antagonists alternately. He'd floor one of them, and then the other. One would try to catch him from behind, but Mizoo was shrugging them off like raindrops off a duck.

Ken stood hypnotized, still dazed from his fighting, unable to move, until he saw an upraised knife come arcing down toward Mizoo's unprotected arm. It galvanized him into action.

Leaping across the area, he grabbed the wrist holding the knife, before it could strike again. Placing his knee in the small of the assailant's back, and using the wrist hold for leverage, he pulled the shiv artist over on his back. Ken dropped his shinbone across the man's throat, and there, sparkling in the dim light, not an inch from the fallen man's head, was a nice, friendly, empty, wine bottle. Ken grabbed for it, smashing it across the head of the man. He felt go limp beneath him. With an aching sigh that seemed to come from his toes, he got to his feet again.

With the broken neck of the bottle he had used, still clenched tightly in his hand, he watched Mizoo make short work of his opponent. While the stocky bullwhip was handling the job, the man that had been kneed in the groin, started to stir around a little, but it took just two well placed kicks in the head to make him sleep soundly again. As Ken turned from that chore, Mizoo buried a left hand to the wrist, in the belly of the man he had chosen, and he fell to his face on the ground. Mizoo backed away, his forearm streaming blood from the cut. He walked slowly over to Ken, laying his bloody arm across Ken's shoulder, the breath wheezing through his broken nose.

"Thanks, Pal, you're a lot tougher than you look. Three of 'em. And cold as butchered hogs in a meat house."

"You weren't bad yourself. And I thought you'd sold out."

"No. I knew what the son-of-a-bitch was going to pull. I know these guys. Seen 'em around before. They make their livin' jack-rollin' drunks in L.A. They work in a team. I was waitin' for 'em."

"Damn right you were."

"Where they fouled up, was waitin' too long. They waited 'til you had their buddy laid out, then they jumped you. They shoulda closed in when the first guy decked you. When you were winded from that kick in the gut. That's when I expected 'em."

"How's the arm? Where the guy cut you."

Mizoo held it up and looked at the wound. It was a ragged tear, bleeding profusely.

"Oh, yeah. That. I'd forgotten all about it. Where's the bastard that gimme the cold steel?"

"That's him, with the cut on his head."

Grimly, Mizoo took the broken, jagged neck of the bottle that Ken held in his hand, and walked over to the prostrate form of the knife handler. He jabbed the glass into his cheek, giving the bottle a half turn, with his strong wrist, delighting in the feel of tearing flesh under his hand. When he had finished his mutilation, he threw the glass against the side of the building.

"That'll make that son-of-a-bitch think twice, before he slices any more Missouri meat. Let's get the hell out of here."

"We've got to get that arm of yours fixed up."

"Hell, it's not too tough. How about you?"

"I'm okay now. I don't know how I'll feel tomorrow."

"Okay, then. We'll go to my place, stick a bandage on my arm, and continue this party. The night's still a pup."

"I can't go any place in these clothes. They're all ripped up and probably got blood and stuff, all over them."

Mizoo laughed.

"Don't worry about it. You can get some clean stuff at my place. They'll fit you a little short, but what the hell. Who's going to notice that, in the joints we're going to. I'll give you a shirt and some jeans. It's my Christmas present to you."

"Well, thanks."

"Think nothin' of it. Now, let's go inside and get our beer and get movin'."

"My lips are too puffed up to put a beer glass against them."

"Horse crap. Do 'em good. The cold'll take the swelling down."

Ken was still no nearer his goal. He hadn't tied up with a woman yet, and he had to find one, get sacked in, and then furnish a witness, a co-respondent of Connie's divorce action. And it was getting later all the time. Ten after ten, now.

All the eyes in the place fastened on them in dead silence as they walked across the room to the table on which their quart beer bottles stood. The girl stared at them in horrified fascination, as they approached her, her eyes widening still more, as Mizoo leaned gently toward her, cupping her left breast with his hand, wet with blood that was draining down his arm from the slash. Kissing her long and tenderly, as she sat paralyzed. A great glob of red stained her white blouse, over the rising mound, tempting and delicious, that Mizoo had caressed.

"Don't look so scared, Sweetheart. We didn't kill 'em. Your boy friend and his buddies are just taking a little nap out in the alley."

Ken's right eye was beginning to turn blue.

10:15 P.M.

THE LONG HALL of the gilt and blue picture palace was a mass of chatter as the light fixtures on the wall came glowing on for the three minute intermission, that would enable the management to further fill their pockets, selling sweets, between features.

People swarmed the aisles, carrying enough rations of one kind and another, to feed a snowbound village. Children made a sprint track of the aisle, racing from the top rear door in a mad dash for the stage, knocking into a precariously laden commuter or two, causing popcorn to fly in a blizzard of kernels.

Connie shifted, turning to Gladys, who was idly eating mints.

"When we were kids, they didn't have all this junk for you to eat during the show, did they, Glad?"

"They had it all right, hon, but the picture business didn't have it sewed up. There always used to be a malt shop, or a drugstore, right next to the movie, and they had penny candy and jawbreakers, and you'd stop in and buy everything in sight, before you went to the show. There wasn't these crazy intermissions just so you could make the rich movie people richer."

"And they're just like everything else these days. They don't give you anything for your money. That last picture wasn't so bad, but it seems like everywhere you go, they've got a Western."

"I wonder why that is?" Gladys said.

"I guess it's caused by transition. Remember those awful 'B' flag-wavers we got during the war? Well, now they've got no excuse to show those things, and horse operas and gangster pictures is all they've got."

"Yeah, I guess you're right."

Gladys subsided into silence, and once more Connie's reservoir of self-pity filled. She sat there, in the midst of the shrieking cacophony around her, and brooded on what had come to pass that evening. The episode with the box, that brassy blonde with the ridiculous glasses, standing at her door, saying those familiar things about Ken. At least, he had been her Ken. That was just one of the things that would be changed after tonight. Her entire way of life would be changed; her parents would never want her to enter their house again, would never want to acknowledge her as their daughter. Even Gladys, sitting there so bovinely patient, might not care to claim her as a friend.

But it was something she had to do. Ken, feeling about her the way he did, must be given his freedom. She loved him so that it ached deep inside, making it almost impossible to swallow, and the thing she must do must be completed soon, before her fluttering will vanished completely, and she came crawling back to him on her knees.

She surely wasn't going to find a partner for her crime here.

"Glad?"

"Mmmm?"

"Do you really want to stay for the next feature?"

"But it's just going to start in a second."

"It isn't so important, is it?"

"It's the one we came to see. I didn't come just for that Western."

"But it still isn't too good a picture, is it?"

"Connie. Glen Ford's my boy, a real lover. Well, he's not a real romantic lover like Ty Power, but he's cute. I like to see him."

"I can't use a make-believe lover tonight."

"What do you mean?"

"I mean something in the flesh. At least, to get out of this show. I feel so restless tonight. I can't stand to sit inside, cooped up in this little box."

"What kind of ideas do you have, Con?"

"Well, let's go somewhere and dance."

"Don't be silly, hon. We don't have any escorts. We couldn't just go barging in some place, and commandeer a couple of fellows. And, anyway, what about Ken? This is a switch for you, isn't it?"

"Ken doesn't seem to think the fact that he's married should hold him down any. So why should it stop me? A man makes out all right, when he goes some place stag. Why can't a woman?"

"It's just a man's world. You've got to accept that. You sure you don't want to stay for the second feature?"

"That's the point I was trying to get across."

"All right, Connie. Don't jump on me because you've got a grudge against Kenny. If you want to go out and roast the town tonight, I'm game to go along for the laughs."

"You know where we could go, have a few drinks, have some fun, without having to depend on a man to take us, maul us around, and bring us home?"

"I thought, by the tone of your voice, that you could stand a little mauling around."

"I don't know yet just what I do want tonight. But I do know that if I sit in this show another minute, I'll scream."

They stood up and began pushing their way to the aisle, lunging by protruding knees, tramping on someone's toes, unseeing in the dark. People were craning around them to see the cast and credits of the beginning picture.

"All right, all right, honey. Don't get in a panic. We'll go. When you get your mind made up, you're like a steam train," Gladys said.

"I just want to get going."

"You ever been on the town?"

"You mean, out on the prowl?"

"Same thing. Watch your step, 'cause there's plenty of fellows that are looking for girls like you, and they play for keeps. They'll do anything to get you up in their apartment."

"Maybe I'll do anything to get there."

Gladys frowned.

"Don't talk silly, Connie. You're married, and Kenny's a nice guy, even though he has fouled you up, somehow. Give him a chance and you'll get back together."

"Maybe I don't want to get back."

"What's gotten into you? You're really bitter."

"That doesn't matter now. Let's just be on our way."

"Well, I'm going to stick close, 'cause I'd feel guilty if anything happened to you. I'd feel it was my fault."

"For instance, what could happen?"

"Oh, you know. You could go off with some fellow. Go out in a car, or something. Like that Dahlia girl. Look what happened to her. I'll bet she didn't know she was going to get stabbed and killed that way, when she went out with that fellow."

"No, she probably didn't. But only a fool lets that happen to her. If a girl keeps her wits about her, she can usually control a man."

"I wouldn't say so all the time. What about Ken? Did you control him today? Something must have happened, or you wouldn't be so mad at him."

"Ken's different."

"Oh."

When they got to the parking lot, Gladys slid under the wheel of her car, lighting a cigarette and handing one to Connie, who leaned luxuriously back on the seat, allowing her firm, ripe breasts to push tightly against her light blouse. A deep inhalation of smoke coursed her lungs, and with a heavy breath, it ran from her mouth, like water from a river.

"Got any ideas?" she asked Gladys.

"Yes, I think so. There's a hotel in Pasadena, with the cutest little bar. Some pretty fat bank accounts get in there, too. I think it's about as nice a place as any. And they're not particular about unescorted women. As far as they know, we might be paying guests, and they can't afford to insult us, can they?"

"You know all the angles, don't you? And you were giving me a sermon. Who are you trying to fool?"

"I'll admit I've been picked up a few times, but it's different with me. I don't have anyone to account to. But I will, if you get into any trouble. Ken knows you're out with me tonight, and I wouldn't want anything to happen."

"What's going to happen? What if I do find someone I'd like to go to bed with. I'll do it, that's all. That doesn't mean I'm going to run away to Europe with him. Nor does it mean that I'll spend all Christmas week in bed in a hotel room. I'm just going to make it quick. Do the thing that Ken seems so good at."

"I don't care how you run your life, Connie, no matter how good a friend you are, but I want you to be careful, to size the fellow up pretty carefully, before you do anything silly. There's an awful lot of funny guys around lately. They look just like anybody else, but they don't get their kicks in the usual way. Perverts. A girl could get killed fooling with those guys."

"I don't think you'd have to worry about that, if you kept your head and looked the fellow over carefully, before you went out with him. You can usually tell when a man's a little off. They don't talk about the right things, or something will give you the clue."

"It's easy for you to say. You've never been around fellows very much. Who have you ever gone out with besides Kenny?"

"Oh, I've been out with other men. Kenny's not the only one I've ever known."

"The only other one was Rich, at the plant, during the war, and he played you for a sap, from what I heard. You've been going with Kenny since you knew the difference between boy and girl. I don't want you to get mad, but you know as well as I do, that most men are no good at all."

It was obvious that Gladys was familiar with the neighborhood, because although the curbs were filled with parked cars, she swerved into a back alley, and snugged the car up against the back of a billboard, in a pitch black cul-de-sac. The girls stepped out, throwing their coats around their shoulders.

"You want to lock it, Glad?"

"Better. There's a lot of Mexican kids that roam around here at night, and they'll swipe anything they can get their hands on."

"Okay, hon. You get the doors on that side, and I'll get them on this."

They strolled easily along Colorado Street, and it was lined with spangled shop windows, ornately decorated, a come-on, like so many other holidays that have come to mean nothing more than a time of profit for the merchant. The season heralded in with the blare and fanfare of a highly specialized advertising campaign, full page ads and cuts, higher prices for everything, from staples to toys, and every loose grifter in town out on the boulevard to make a mark.

"How much farther do we have to walk to this place?" Connie asked.

"Just around the next corner."

"What's it like? Is it nice?"

"Uh-huh. It's got a little bar, with ferns and palms and stuff around it, and a lot of tables and booths. They serve meals there any time you want them. And a little five piece orchestra that plays, and you can dance."

Now that the time to really crash through the wall of her reserve had come, Connie had a tight, frightened feeling in her stomach. How to act, what to say, would come naturally, she supposed, but still she didn't like the idea of putting herself on the block, so to speak, for a few drinks and a dance or two. Actually, when you got right down to it, this was a form of prostitution.

Selling your body for an evening's entertainment. And yet, you could look at it another way. If the act of having a man was the end, in itself, instead of merely a means to an end, the person was giving away an evening's time to attain sexual satisfaction. Why had she been forced into such a dirty, rotten compromise? She felt as though there was an inch of grime over her entire body. Still, if she was going to carry out her plan, and it did seem the only solution to her problem, she would enter into this game of catch me and conquer me, with no hesitation and no regrets. If she used her head, nothing could go wrong. She felt a little nauseated, it was true, but it was silly to be frightened of a new experience like this. She was a woman, and had all the equipment she needed to play the game.

Gladys and her talk of perverts would scare a prostitute.

The bar was beautiful, when they got inside. The strains of music wafted toward them, as they went into the lounge to check their faces. A touch here and there, with a dab of lipstick, and she was ready to face anyone. She gazed, for a moment, at her reflection in the glass; eyes a bit too mournful, she decided, something like a starved beagle hound, and that would never do. She could never attract anyone that way. A stroke of mascara, and a feeble smile, framed by carmined lips. Her contrasting raven hair that cascaded to her shoulders in a drooping wave, and now she was beautiful enough for any man. She had nothing to be afraid of, and she stood proudly erect in front of the glass to prove it to herself. She decided her breasts looked tempting enough, rising full orbs that swelled in perfection to their apex, and her nipples had hardened in anticipation, so that you could see a suggestion of shadow on her slip, through her diaphanous blouse.

"Satisfied?" Gladys asked.

"Think I'll do?"

"You'll knock 'em dead, kid."

Connie held up crossed fingers.

"Here goes nothing."

They skirted the dance floor, seating themselves in a booth not too far from the band. After a few moments, the bar-girl, in a brief, simulated Western costume, stood before them, her order pad ready.

"I'll have a Ginger High," Connie said.

"No, you won't," Gladys interrupted. "Make that two Singapore Slings, honey."

After the waitress had gone, Connie flared.

"What's the matter with a Ginger High? We always fix them at home."

"Wait a sec, Con. These drinks are costing us money. Our money, and we haven't got too much to spend. If you don't drink at a steady rate in these places, they give you the old eye, and that means you're a cheap piker. Wait 'til we start drinking on some fellow's money, and then you can have anything your little heart desires."

"So what? What's this Singapore Sling business?"

"You know what they are. But you don't recognize the name. They come in a glass about a foot high, and they're pink, made out of Sloe Gin. Not too hard to take, and they last longer than anything else. You take Momma's advice, and you won't have too long to wait. Not with the face and figure you're wearing tonight."

The music rose behind them with a rattle of the maracas and a throb of tom-toms; a catchy rumba to start the hips weaving. Connie drummed in time to the rhythm, with the palm of her hand on the table. Her shoulders swayed to the beat, and her breasts moved, just a fraction later.

"Honey, you're really eager. See what you married gals miss."

"I'm just in the mood tonight."

"Does Ken ever take you out to spots like this?"

"We never seem to go any place. Either I'm busy, or he is, or no money."

"Well, wives are rarely seen here, except with some other man. Mostly people on the loose, in one way or another, looking for some laughs to make them forget every day."

"You're quite a philosopher, Glad. Where'd you get all the deep thoughts."

"I see life."

The waitress arrived with the tall glasses, precariously balanced on a tiny tray. Gladys dug a bill out of her wallet and tossed it on the table.

"These girls act like they're doing you a favor to bring you a drink," Gladys said, after the waitress had gone. "And did you see the look on her face? Wouldn't that stifle you? They hate to serve girls sitting alone, because they know they'll never get a tip."

Connie nodded.

"Got a cigarette?"

Gladys extended the pack, glancing over her shoulder at the crowd.

"I guess we haven't been seen yet. Or else, there isn't a wolf in the crowd with gumption enough to come over and ask us to dance."

"Maybe we're not their type."

"Don't be silly. Just being a member of the opposite sex makes us automatically their type. The guys that hang out here."

"Maybe they like either blondes or brunettes. Most men have their preferences."

"The choice is which one looks easier to get in bed. With no strings attached. Which one looks the more gullible. Talk about a woman's intuition. These guys really travel the beam when it comes to figuring women. But I usually try to have a few surprises for them along the way."

"You mean to tell me that after all your talk, you've never gone in the hay with one of these fellows? I've heard you tell me about some of the nights. I know better, Glad."

Gladys took a deep drag on her cigarette.

"Oh, hell, no. I wouldn't kid you, hon. I've been had plenty, but only when I've wanted to, and on my terms. There's no use getting tangled up with a goof that thinks just because he has a girl, it's true love and something to last forever, with vine-covered cottages and babies and that kind of stuff. If I wanted to get married and be tied down with a raft of kids, the rest of my life, I might as well hold up a bank and get put in jail."

"You mean you wouldn't get married, if the right man comes along?"

"There is no right man. They're all a bunch of egotistical idiots. No, Connie, the only way to do it is to get some guy that has a little dough, and is really on the ball, quiet, competent, and knows how to love. Then, give yourself to him—go all out, no reservations—give him all you've got. Then you have the urge out of your system for awhile, and you've still shared something beautiful with someone."

"Where does love and romance come in? The way you sound to me, you don't believe in sex as any more than a kind of soiled, biological duty to yourself."

"Sometimes, you will run into an egghead in a place like this, that still believes that woman is an unsullied, pure virgin, descended directly from heaven, and should be accorded every courtesy and remain untouched in a sanitary glass case. They forget that we have the same emotions and feelings, drives and urges that they do, and that secretly, we want, when we come into a bar by ourselves, the same thing they do."

A beige sport coat, garnished with a bright, plaid bow tie, was tapping on Gladys' shoulder, trying to get her attention, to shut off the flow of words.

"What's that, Glad?" Connie asked.

"Later, hon. We've got company."

"Hey, blondie," Sport Coat said, "How about bending the body?"

"Remember what I said, Connie? It looks like I'm the easy one."

Sport Coat looked puzzled.

"What's that, friend?"

"Just telling my friend one of my childhood secrets. Merry Christmas."

"Same to you, and to you too, honey. C'mon, Blondie, let's dance."

"I just love these personality boys. Such fire, such poise, such crust."

"Don't be bitter. Let's go."

"Okay. See you later, Connie. Keep an eye on my bag, there's a good girl."

Connie sipped at her drink for a few moments, staring at the empty face of the wooden wall before her, her mood closing in. The smoke laden air seemed to pulse in the dim light around her, and her thoughts went out in desperation to Kenny, wherever he might be. It was very hard for her to do this thing. She had been forced into it, but why had Kenny crowded her into this situation? Had he no more use for her, after she had waited and prayed for him, these past years? True, they didn't get to see as much of one another, as they might, but she did have certain responsibilities toward her friends, that had stood by her so staunchly, when her whole life seemed to collapse with Kenny's induction. And now, it was hard to make the old values mean anything. The things that had held the two of them together. The insignificant details of living that had meant so much, the first few months of their marriage, no longer had importance. They were just dull cogs to function in the daily routine.

The insurmountable fact was, that Kenny no longer cared. The sooner he was rid of her, the happier he'd be. It was a complete hell of a world.

Suddenly, she became conscious that a man had slipped into her booth, and was sitting in Gladys' seat, across from her. His face was long, with craggy lines, topped by a shock of black hair, and his eyes, deep, dark, were boring into her.

"Oh, you frightened me for a second," Connie stammered. "I didn't see you sit down. How long have you been there?"

"Just a second or two," he said, in a low, deliciously masculine voice. "I was just curious as to why a pretty girl like you had to be unhappy on Christmas Eve. Do you realize that in just a little more than an hour, it will be Christmas?"

"It will, won't it? I hadn't thought about it."

"What is Santa Claus going to leave in your stocking?"

"Oh, I don't know. The usual things, I guess."

"Would you care to dance? That's my real reason for coming over. But you were so intent on that glass in front of you, I couldn't catch your eye."

Connie stood up, arranging her skirt over her hips.

"Just daydreaming, I guess. No real trouble."

"I often do that. But never at night, just during working hours. On company time."

"Don't tell me you have to work for a living. I thought everyone who came to places like this were above all that sort of thing."

She gave him her right hand, stepping into his arms for the waltz, the band was playing. He guided her out into the center of the lazily, gyrating dancers, with competent ease, the palm of his hand strong and warm against her back.

"Oh, yes, I work. But everyone has to have a hobby. I drink."

"That's a different hobby. Not quite like stamp collecting, is it?"

"Not quite. But you'd be surprised how widespread my hobby is. Some even have it for a full time vocation, but very few admit it."

"Don't you find it expensive?"

"Not as costly as marriage."

"Don't you believe in marriage?"

"Not any more. Once bitten, twice shy."

"Then at least, you've given it a try."

"Oh yes, but the poor girl couldn't reconcile herself to sharing me with my other hobby."

"I think you're just kidding me."

"God love me, I'm not, dear lady. My late departed wife was a veritable shrew. Departed for Reno, that is."

"Where did you pick up that Shakespearian dialect?"

"I just kid around with it. Actually, this world could use a little more of that kind of thing. Chivalry and all the other things are so frightfully dead."

"Maybe, if you had been a little more genteel, your wife might not have left you."

"You mean, if I hadn't been so genteel with her lovers, she would have toed the line. I'm only an accountant in a bank, and some of the fellows I found in the house were too big for me. I'm what they call a live coward, and besides, by that time, I didn't care very much anyway."

"If you really loved her, you must have cared."

"That's just it. I didn't love her any more. I figured that if she wanted to run around, no amount of beating or pleading was going to make her stop. She just didn't love me, and nothing that I could do would change it."

"That makes sense."

The music died off on a single chord, and they stopped and stood apart. He was staring at the beauty of her, and she, unaware of his scrutiny, looked around the floor for Gladys and her brightly clad partner.

"I don't know why I'm loading all my troubles off on you," he said, trying to regain her attention, "when I'm sure you have plenty of your own."

"I don't mind." She smiled. "It takes me out of myself and makes me realize that I'm not the only one in the world."

He had a slanting half smile that brought Kenny to her mind with painful clarity. His manner was somewhat like Ken's; the ego there for all to see, but skillfully camouflaged behind a self-deprecating manner. It wouldn't do for her to get involved with someone that made her think of Kenny. It would hurt too much.

"You are probably the prettiest girl in the whole world, on this Christmas Eve," he said, smoothly, in a tone that told her he was joking in a manner that he wanted taken seriously.

"I'll bet you say that to all beautiful women."

"Who's got all the conceit in your family?"

"I have. Whom did you think?"

The saxaphone picked up the tempo for a faster fox trot, but Connie was disappointed, as her partner's feet, lagging on the beat, got in the way of her dancing. Try as she might, she couldn't follow his step.

"It's my fault," he apologized. "I can waltz and do the conservative steps. I'm no jazz artist. I can't jitterbug."

It was then, that Connie became completely disinterested in this particular specimen. Now that she was able to survey him objectively, instead of from the first flush of gratitude at having rescued her from facing Gladys' triumphant march back to the table, unhonored, unspoken and unsung. She faced several glaring faults in her partner now. Or rather, her rationalizing mind supplied her with reasons as to why he was much too small for this season's fishing. She would throw him back in the pond, and wait for something larger.

She said, after a moment, "Are you anxious to get back to your highball?"

"There is that angle. I hadn't thought of it, but they do evaporate so quickly."

"Then, if you'll just escort me to my table.... "

"Certainly, dear lady."

When she was seated, Connie mused that after all, if she was out on the prowl, looking for some ape to take the rap in court with her, she might as well get as good looking and rich a fellow as possible. Not only would it be more convincing, but what would Kenny think if he had to drag in some homely jerk and insist that this throwback had seduced his wife and alienated his affections. It would be a blow to his pride.

What a silly fool she was. She sipped her drink, and allowed herself, once more, to be washed up on the bleached, hopeless sands of despair.

Finally, the music stopped, and the sport coat brought Gladys back to the table. They were giggling as they crossed the floor, and their laughter was maddening to Connie who wished to be left alone in her misery.

"Hey, Con," Gladys was still ten feet from the table. "This is Donnie. You remember Donnie Racci, played on the 'B's' for East campus of Pasadena in '39, when we were Juniors."

The name wandered around in her brain, lonely, with no associations, until it came knocking, begging to be let out.

"Nope," she shook her head. "It doesn't do anything to me."

Gladys and Donnie slid across the slick leather on the other side of the booth.

"Well, he did, anyway." Gladys pouted and then turned to Donnie. "How come we never met you when you went to Muir?"

"Hell, honey, I don't know. You know how it is in school. You don't even see the kids in the class under you. And I had other connections that year."

"Listen to him talk."

"How about a drink around?" he said. "What are you having?"

"V.O. and ginger," Gladys said, promptly.

"Same." Connie nodded.

"You don't say much, do you?" Donnie said, handing around the cigarettes.

Connie stared at the table, idly swirling the dwindling ice cubes around in her empty glass. She didn't bother to look up at him.

"Leave her be. She's got man trouble," Gladys said.

"Just lose one?"

"I don't know what the story is. I'm just an innocent bystander. And that's only half the story. I don't want to know. I haven't got nose trouble."

"Meaning I have?"

"No. No, Donnie boy. I mean nothing of the kind. I just don't know, and I'm not aiming to find out. And that's the way it is."

The gabble of words went skimming over Connie's head, like wild geese in flight, and she took no more notice of it, than if she were a rainbow trout in the lake below.

Donnie was saying, "But, hell, Gladys. This is Christmas Eve. I just like to see everybody have a good time on Christmas Eve."

"Oh, leave her alone for a minute or two. She's singing the blues to herself. She'll snap out of it, if you just leave her be for a minute."

"Okay, hon, whatever you say. You're the boss."

And the smoke bit into Connie's lungs and went sweeping out in a sweet, cleaning motion, and still the ice cubes, as tiny as corn kernels now, went running, running, around the bottom of the glass, and one was herself. Now he was chasing her, and then she chasing him, and they were trapped by the transparent walls of life, and the more they fought against it and each other, the more they were worn down by their surrounding environment, and the smaller they got inside, the faster they had to run to cover the same distance, and the faster they ran, the smaller. . . .

11:00 P.M.

THIS PLACE was much as the last; the same smoke and din, the same raggy music from a piano that hadn't been tuned since the day Moses brought the tablets down the mountain, the only change being that here he was flanked by a guitar man and a man that played the traps. You couldn't honestly say he was a drummer, because all he had was a trap drum and he rattled it in time to the music, as though he was part of the American Legion Drum and Bugle Corps, marching down Main Street on Armistice Day.

The place was long, narrow, with a concrete floor for dancing that was bisected by a long, gleaming shuffleboard. Dancers jerked themselves around the tiny area, in jeans and cotton dresses, valiantly trying to keep in step. They looked like a plague of St. Vitus had broken out among them.

Mizoo had loaned him a T-shirt and a pair of Levis, and now that the beer had started to soak into some of the cracks in his frame, and to build up a backlog of warmth, he felt more at ease than he had in his suit, trying to fool all the Okies that he wasn't really a city boy, just by leaving off his tie.

His suit was a wreck. He'd seen it in the light, when he got to Mizoo's place, and he'd also taken a good look at himself in the glass in the bathroom, while he was tying up Mizoo's arm. He was in about the same shape as the suit. One of the lapels was nearly ripped off. The pocket was hanging by a couple of threads, and both knees were tattered and frayed. His good, white shirt; he only had one more like it, had some drops of blood on it from his split lip. Either he had bitten it himself, or the perforation had occurred under the impact of that first straight left to the face that had laid him on his back. Anyway, the lip was as big as a house and sore as a boil.

There was a groove, shining whitely against the brown, in the leather of his shoes, where he must have cut it against glass, and his right eye was puffed up, and would swell even more, before the night was over. It was just starting to discolor.

After they had gotten the blood sponged away, they discovered that the cut on Mizoo's arm was not as bad as Kenny had thought. Tape and bandage, used freely, had covered the wound, and Mizoo was eager to go.

"C'mon, Pal. Let's fly low. How do you feel?"

"I think I survived."

"And did damn well, too. Those guys will have knots on their heads like turkey eggs, tomorrow. That'll teach 'em to mess with Mizoo and his buddies."

Self-satisfaction, and an excusable effluvium of ego, filled Ken, and he was glad that he had shown up well in front of Mizoo, who was as strong as a bull, and as feisty as a terrier.

And so, the next stop on Mizoo's route, a real snatch patch, as he called it, was this smoky, noise-filled hole in the wall, named, appropriately enough, "Crazy Casey's." And he was getting to that filled-to-bloating stage, the glow coming through to him, like the new word of the gospel. The people around him, none of whom had spoken a sound to him, were all his new found friends, and going to do wonders for them, if only he knew what he could do.

"Drink up," Mizoo said.

"Anything you say."

"Let's get lined up. It's gettin' late."

"See any possibilities?"

"A couple. But let's have another beer first."

"Anything you say."

"You're damned agreeable tonight."

"I figure I've been in enough fights tonight. What do you think?"

"I reckon. Hey, Mac. Two more."

Ken gazed around the room, taking in the tinsel and spangles, hanging in the smoke, like stalactites in a dim cave, and the faded crepe paper bells and other visible evidence that it was Christmas Eve, and a time to be merry and gay, and all the rest of it, but sometimes it was hard to remember, when you were too busy searching for something else.

He wondered which women Mizoo had in mind.

"You goin' to pay for this round?" Mizoo asked. "I'm just about out of dough."

"Sure. Why not?"

"Never mind, boys," the bartender smiled, running a damp rag over the scarred counter. "This one's on the house. Merry Christmas."

"Thanks. Merry Christmas to you, too. And all your friends and relatives."

They clinked the glasses together.

"Hey, Mizoo?" Ken asked, lazily. It was warm, snug and warm, in this long slot of a hall, after driving through the velvet air outside, finishing the beer they had brought from the scene of the fight, and the few shots of bourbon they had had at Mizoo's house.

"Yeah?"

"If we're after the women, how come we don't buy a quart like we did in the last place?"

"The gals I got in mind, already have a couple quarts. I'm figurin' on latchin' on to some of their rations."

Kenny made a silent round "oh" with his lips, and nodded.

"Okay, Pal, let's move in."

"Not so fast, Ken boy. You got to work smooth. You're the prettiest. You ask one of 'em to dance."

"What's the matter with you asking one of them?"

"I can't dance, and besides I take too many ugly pills. Them two over there, in the last booth. The young chick and that older babe with her."

"Okay. Then, what do you do?"

"After you have yourself in solid, I'll just mosey over and you'll introduce me as your long lost buddy-buddy, and I'll ace myself in, and we'll just be one big happy family."

Ken nodded and slid off his stool. The air was murky with smoke, and it was like swimming through a thick fog, clearing the people away from in front of him, on the dance floor, by continued sweeps of his long arms. His yellow blond hair was fluffed on his head, and flattened by coursing fingers, and his eye was discolored and the split lip hurt like hell. He had no confidence in himself. No self-respecting girl would give him a second look, especially in the little ensemble he was wearing. The T-shirt showed how thin he was by highlighting his corrugating ribs, and the old jeans that Mizoo had worn so long, they had gone powder blue in the knee, were too short for him. He was no salesman, but he'd try.

One of the women was quite a way down the road with the wrong kind of load. She sat loose in the seat, hanging grimly onto a glass of beer and a cigarette. She was older than the girl that faced her across the table. Big in body, bone and bust, which was all that Ken could see, with a mess of what had once been red hair, but during recent years, had darkened to an off shade of brown. The flesh on the face was not as firm as it once was, just beginning to slough off the jowls, but she could still stop them in a crowd and have them look at her, if she was careful about pancake and mascara and lipstick, and the rest. She looked to be on the shady side of forty.

She was listening to the other babe yakity yak, and Ken decided that the one with the flapping mouth was the one for him, although she seemed a more formidable beachhead to land on, with the independent shadow of her jawline, and the dark, burning intensity of her eyes, showing that she would have more defenses than her older companion.

The visible portion of the younger girl seemed like a model's dream, and she didn't seem aware that she had a bust line that overshadowed the beer glass she held in her hand. Her head was topped with straight, severe hair, drawn back over her ears. Her skin was magnolia, the color of a petal that has just started to turn, and there was that faint suggestion of contempt for the human race in general, and the opposite sex, in particular, that made you want to get in there and rut around and make her change her mind. But there was that "no nonsense, please" manner, and Kenny was just a little afraid to tackle this formidable creature.

What the hell, boy, all she can say is, no. She can't eat you.

He stood at the side of their table with his thumbs hooked in his Levi pockets, until the young one finished her little speech.

"… And that no 'count Jim Mitchell, runnin' round with that Jezebel, spendin' his money right on the nail keg buyin' pretties for that gal, while his wife and young 'uns sits home with nary a bite in their poor bellies. Hit ain't right for a woman to have to put up with sich. But you know as well as I do that Millie Mitchell ain't got the gumption of a frog, or she'd'a slapped him behind the ears with a hickory club afore now."

It was painful to listen to that high, twanging whine, straight out of the sand flat country. Apparently, the girl's companion thought so, too.

"Hell, honey, we ain't taken the Mitchell's to raise. What do you care what the hell they do? If Millie hasn't got the sand to stand up on her own two feet, more fool she. I got mine trained, and he hasn't stepped out of line for fear I'll find it out. Anyway, what do you know about it? You ain't got a man and probably never will, the way you treat 'em."

This was a different voice, seeming vibrantly young, to come from such an aging face. It was low and lazy. The tone seemed to drift into your very insides and flood it with depth and unimagined meaning.

Ken cleared his throat to announce his presence, but the whine started again.

"Well, if Jim Mitchell is a sample of the men, I'll take rabbits."

"Don't put your faith in rabbits. They tomcat around a lot more than men."

"You're the one to preach. Ever' time Tom goes away on a trip, you bed down with some stranger."

"Goddamn you, you stinking virgin-talking bitch. I have reasons for what I do. I used to be waiting patiently, until I found out what Tom does on those trips. He never sleeps alone. Why'n hell should I? Ten years ago, I'd'a snatched your hair out, but now, what the hell do you know about life? Have you ever lived? Besides, this child has only a few good years left."

Ken thought it was either time to break in with his little speech, or go back to the bar and sit down. Forget about the whole thing.

Then he thought of the look of derision that he would see in the eyes of Mizoo. For some unutterable reason, he wanted to show up well in front of Mizoo. There was some kind of drawing, demanding quality in Mizoo's personality. He was such a stocky, cocky guy, that you instinctively wanted to show him up, although you knew you never would, because no matter what the facts were, he would never accept them, until they were overwhelmingly in his favor. It went even further. Such facts just didn't exist for him. They were fourth dimensional. An unknown dialectic in time.

He had better maneuver. He reached out and touched the younger one, who was drinking in hurt silence, after her companion's last remark.

"Dance?" he asked.

She got up, without a word, and slid out of the booth. The other woman watched the two of them, drawing on her cigarette, fixing Ken with her eyes, as though he were a frog pinned to a board in a laboratory, and she was about to remove his brain with a couple of surgical blades and pop it in a jar of formaldehyde.

They slid into the squirming humanity around them, and though it was hard to talk to the jigging rhythm, Ken managed to start a conversation.

"You come here often?" he asked.

"Sometimes." She rationed the word out, as though she grudged parting with it.

"Always with your friend there?"

The granite jaw lifted a little and shifted, just a fraction in his direction. Her eyes were like flint chips and they impaled him.

"That friend is my aunt. I come with her some, and times I come with others."

"That's nice to know. I'll bet you lead a hell of a life."

"I get along." She stiffened away from him. Not enough to disturb their dancing, but he knew that the artillery had him zeroed in, and there would be nothing left, but a smoking shell crater, if he tried to put one foot on the beach.

"I'll bet you do at that. If they make a pass at you, honey, I'll bet you crush their spines for 'em."

"They'll wish they hadn't. Get the idea?"

"It's beginning to seep through."

"You're too damn pretty. You're a pretty boy. All you pretty boys are all the damn same. You think you're God's gift to females. Well, not this one."

"I'm not worried about you, my little prairie flower. There's plenty of fish in the ocean, and I've thrown back better one's than you."

"You're pretty smart, aren't you?"

"I get along," Ken mimicked.

"Smart guy."

"You're just bitter."

"I ought to leave you right here on the floor. Leave you standin', with your mouth flappin' like a tater sack."

"You wouldn't do a thing like that." Ken's voice was weighted with sarcasm. "It wouldn't be ladylike."

"I ain't a damn lady, and I don't like you. And I don't care who knows it."

She stepped away from him, as though to walk off the floor and leave him standing, but the timing was in Ken's favor, because, at that moment the music stopped and the band stood up to take a break. Ken followed the girl to her table.

The older woman smiled at him, as he approached.

"How'd you make out, Carol? Does he dance good?" The aunt asked.

"I'm afraid your niece got a little upset. I hurt her precious feelings," Ken said, smoothly.

"Oh, hell, that happens all the time. She can be nice sometimes, but mostly, she's just a spoiled brat. An opinionated, snot-nosed, stuck-up little brat."

"I am, like hell," Carol flared. "If I am, you're a damn sight worse, runnin' around ever' time your old man goes out of town. You askin' me to come out with you, buyin' me drinks, so I'll front for you, and you can look the young fellows over. You're just dreamin' about the past, that's what you're doin'."

"See what I mean," the aunt smiled. "No wonder she ain't got any girl friends left, but me, and no fellow will take her out twice runnin'...."

"An' do you know why?" the girl interrupted. " 'Cause that ol' witch always makes a pass at 'em, that's why. An' can you see a young guy in his right mind goin' for an ol' bag like her?"

"Now is that a way for a young girl to act on Christmas Eve?" The aunt grasped Ken's hand, pulled him down to the bench. "Whyn't you sit down and have some beer with us? It's Christmas Eve and all. C'mon, Blondie, sit down here, and have a drink or two, and a couple laughs. Carol's a little upset, and doesn't mean half what she says, do you, honey?"

Still holding Ken's hand with her left, she leaned drunkenly across the table and stroked Carol's arm, with her right hand.

"Oh, Jesus, here we go again," Carol sighed. "The blood of the unborn lamb."

With surprising strength in her grip, the older woman pulled Ken off balance, until he was forced to sit heavily in the booth beside her.

"I'd like to have a drink with you," Ken stammered, afraid of the whirlpool of emotion that eddied and swirled around him. "I'll be glad to, but I have a friend over at the bar. He's waiting for me."

"Hell. Bring him over. There's always room for one more. We got plenty of beer, and there's more where that came from. He can sit with Carol. Maybe she'll like him better than she does you."

"No, we don't want to break into your party."

"Don't be silly. What kind of a party do you think we can have, without any friends around to drink our health on Christmas Eve. Sing 'Auld Lang Syne,' and all that."

"Aunt Clara, that's next week."

"Hell, this week, next week, what's the difference. Drink, laugh, made love while you can, tomorrow you might be dead."

"That's a hot one," the girl said.

"You shut up, Carol. I'm payin' for this party, and if I want some friends over to have a few drinks and a little fun, I'll invite 'em, and if you don't like it, you can get the hell out and walk home."

"Merry Christmas," said Carol.

The aunt with her old face and young figure ignored the girl and turned to Kenny, boring her breasts into his arm—breasts that apparently were capped by artificial padding, because their rigidity didn't give under pressure, but kept stabbing in. A hank of her reddish brown hair had fallen across her cheek, and she was tugging at his arm insistently.

"C'mon, Blondie, get your friend over here, and we'll sit him alongside Carol there, and see how he makes out. I'll bet he don't, because she's either queer, or frigid, because even though she's a fairly good looker, in a bitchy sort of way, she never gives 'em a tumble. None of 'em."

Carol sat with her glass up to her lips, staring blankly over Ken's shoulder, at the band, coming back to the tiny stand. She was not hearing what was being said about her, deliberately.

Ken saw Mizoo weaving his way through the crowd.

"I don't have to call him. He's on his way over now."

"What's the matter? Is he afraid you'll get raped, if you're out of his sight?"

"Nope, that's not it. He's afraid that if there's any raping going on, he's not going to get to participate."

"That figures."

"Aunt Clara!" The girl banged her glass hard on the table, sloshing beer on the end of her cigarette, lying in the ash tray.

"What's eatin' you, pipsqueak?"

"Do you have to talk so horny with these foreigners?"

"Honey, I keep tellin' you this is Christmas Eve. Ain't nobody foreign on Christmas Eve."

Mizoo stood with his hands on his hips, looking as broad as the side of a barn, with that shirt on, and the white of the bandage peeking from the sleeve. The great hooked nose roamed down his rugged face, like a mountain range across the back of a continent, and the snarled eyebrows arched high above his tiny pig eyes. He said nothing. Just stood there, staring.

Clara pounded Ken on the back, laughing, her cigarette skywriting smoke rings in the motion of the other hand.

"Is this your buddy? God, ain't he ugly. I've seen 'em in my time, but never one with a map like that."

"Oh, yeah, Grandma," Mizoo said, leaning forward, his nose almost pushed into her face. "You're no dream boat yourself."

"I've had my day. But you, you're not even dry behind the ears yet, and you haven't got a chance."

"A chance for what?"

"A chance for any lovin', any life, the real kind, like the fellows whisper about on street corners. 'Cause what woman would go for you in her right mind."

Mizoo stood transfixed, for a split second, before Clara began to laugh. It came from deep inside somewhere, and though Carol sat and stared at her aunt, as though she had suddenly slipped off the deep end, Ken saw the joke and grinned. Finally, Mizoo realized that she had given him more than he could dish out, and tried a smile on for size, too.

"Okay, okay, so you got to me. You don't need to bust a gut."

"No offense." She struggled against the chuckles. "Friends?"

"Sure."

"Sit down by little Miss Sourpuss there. See what you can do to knock some life into her. She's a wet blanket tonight."

Mizoo turned to Carol. "Now that's no way to act on Christmas Eve."

"Don't you start that old crap," Carol said, still staring severely into her beer glass. "We've already been through that one."

Clara tugged at Kenny's sleeve.

"Hey, what's your name?"

"Kenny, and that little guy over there's Mizoo."

"Glad to know you. I'm Clara Bamford, and the silent, brooding beauty over there, is Carol Caffin."

"Merry Christmas, and all that kinda stuff," Mizoo said, leaning toward Carol.

"Okay, okay," she sulked. "Merry Christmas, but I know what you really mean."

"Huh?"

"You mean, now that the season's here, you'd like to make merry. Well, for your information, my name's Carol, and don't forget it."

"What's chewin' on her ass?" Mizoo looked across at Clara.

"She's just got a mad on. Don't pay her no mind," Clara said, turning to Kenny. "What some more beer, Blondie? Where's your glass? We got plenty."

Silently, Ken held his glass and she poured the Eastside into it. After he had taken the first sip, she said, "You and Carol didn't make out so good on the floor. She would rather sulk in her beer. How about you and me tryin' it? I'm a pretty good dancer. If you don't believe me, try me out."

Ken looked down into that old face, and groped for an excuse. She was a pretty good old gal, and it was her beer that they were drinking, even though, if he had his way, he and Mizoo would clear out now, because every minute they wasted with these two, Carol, the young one, who might be worth having, under the proper circumstances, was as sore as a branded goat, and the old one, who wasn't worth having, was so eager for young stuff, it was a little sickening, they robbed themselves of an opportunity to do better, elsewhere. But Mizoo didn't seem to care, and after looking around, everybody seemed pretty well taken care of anyway.

It was too late to do anything else. They had to play this one out for what it was worth, because all the good stuff that might be on the loose, was picked up and picked over, long ago, and there was nothing left but the culls. Like these two. And even if Carol did change her mind, it would be for Mizoo, and he would be stuck with this old bag, with her eagle eyes fastened on him, and he was under the thumb.

The thing that had screwed up was that fight. They had come out all right, but he'd had his suit ruined, and Mizoo had been all cut to Jesus, and they'd had to go to Mizoo's place to clean up. By that time, they'd wasted damn near an hour, and in an hour, there's no telling what they might have done.

"How about it?" Clara tugged at his sleeve. "You gonna dance?"

"Yeah, sure," he said, taking another sip. "You sure this stuff isn't too fast for you?"

"Just try me, Blondie. I'm built for speed and endurance."

"That's a good deal."

Ken stood aside, while Clara got out of the booth and preceded him onto the dime-sized floor. Her waist was like a tree trunk, rising out of generous hips, but it wasn't all flab, as he put his arm around her for the dance. The flesh was hard, and she grasped his hand strongly, pressing herself close to him, and he could feel the false rubber, through her sweater, but he didn't care much, because at least she was someone to talk to, something to do. She tried to lead him around the floor, and for a moment, they stood at an impasse, each trying to lead the other, and then, after an eternal second, she relaxed, and the long climb was over, and the dancing was simple after that.

"You know, you're not bad at all," she said.

"Thanks." He was sorry he couldn't say the same.

"You married?"

"Uh-huh."

"How come you're not out with her tonight? Christmas Eve."

"We had a beef. She went out with a girl friend."

Clara looked up and smiled, as though she had a secret that only she and Ken shared.

"So you went out with the boy friend, eh?"

"Mizoo? I just met him tonight. In a bar. Either I picked him up, or he picked me up. I'm not sure which."

"You, a pick up? I'd never of believed it."

"Not me, Clara. You got me all wrong. I like 'em on the female side."

"I'm a gal that likes the habit too. But my old man's got sand in his crotch."

"Tough."

"Yeah, tough. I like young, married guys. Like to take 'em home with me. Give 'em a little food, a few shots, some laughs, a good time."

"Yeah?"

"Young guys like you."

"How about your husband? What does he think about your bringing guests home?"

"Funny thing. He's never home when they come. Always seems to be away some place. Like tonight."

Oh, God, he thought. The second proposition today. And from this old bundle, too. Well, I've got news for her.

"What about tonight?" he asked.

"He had to go to San Diego over the week end. On a business trip, so he said."

"So?"

"Why'n't you come over? We could have a party. Just you and me."

There it was. Laid out on the line for him to look at. Faced with two choices. To go or not to go. With Mizoo sitting back there in the booth, depending on him for a way home, he couldn't be a chintz and leave. He'd have to take him home first. But anyway, he wouldn't go anywhere with this old face.

They're all alike, with the lights turned out.

Not with Connie to compare her to. Even with the lights out, he'd still know what she looked like. His mind would keep the picture clear before him, etched in detail on the inside wall of his tightly closed eyelids. He wouldn't be able to shut out the hideous irony of the farce he was engaged in.

"I don't think I can make it tonight," he said, after a moment's hesitation.

"C'mon, I got some bourbon in the icebox. We'll play some records and get high, and then, when we get in the mood, we can go bed."

Maybe she wasn't as old as she looked, and maybe she'd be a bargain in the old sack, but what the hell, he wasn't up to a lab course in seduction tonight. And, besides, what would Mizoo say when he found out? Probably laugh like a bull, and ask him when he started taking grandmothers to bed.

"No, I'm too tired tonight. I've got to get home and get a little sleep. Tomorrow's Christmas. Remember?"

"Sure, I remember. I'm celebratin' tonight. But if you don't want to come, I'm not going to push. But, I wish you would. You're pretty. I'd like to have you for my own. My collection. I'd stuff you and mount you on the wall."

"That would be a neat trick."

The music had stopped, and they were slowly drifting back to their table. Clara laughed, as she reached across and got her purse.

"What've you and Carol been doin'?" she asked Mizoo.

"Just sittin' here cussin' at each other."

"That figures. Carol, you want to go to the little girls' room? That beer goes right on through without stoppin' to change color."

Ken sat down beside Mizoo and watched the women weave their way to the rest room, and it was like the room emptying, and they were the only people there, he and Mizoo. Nobody looked at them or spoke to them, and even though she did have that old face and phony young looking body, she was someone to talk and laugh with.

"How you making it, buddy?" he asked.

"Man, that Carol's mean. I don't want to have no truck with her. She's the kind that would make up to you, until she had you right between her legs, and then she'd knife you, and laugh her sides out."

"I'm making out a little better, but I'm sure as hell not bragging about it. Clara asked me to come home with her, shack up tonight."

Just to see what Mizoo would say.

"You could do worse. At least, she'd give you a lot of action. She's got ants in her pants for sure. What'd you tell her?"

"No go. I was too tired. Besides, I couldn't leave you here. I've got to drive you home."

"Hell, I don't live far from here. I can walk home."

"You don't have to. I'm not that hard up."

"Suit yourself. If I was in your shoes, I'd go along with her just to see what an old head is like."

Which just went to show you that you couldn't figure out ahead of time what anybody will say.

"Nope. I don't want any part of her. The hell with women tonight. We're not going to do any good. It's too late. All the good ones are gone."

"What do you want to do then? Head home?"

"I want to get stinking."

"Well, let's get a pint or so, and sit in the car, and beat our gums."

"Sounds great."

The women came back, standing by the table, but they didn't seem to want to sit down. Kenny got up.

Clara motioned him to sit down again, with an elegant gesture, smoke swirling from the cigarette in her fingers.

"No. We got to go. Carol's been bitchin' at me again, and I guess I better get her home, before she pops her cork. You guys finish the beer. Carol don't want me to drink no more."

As she leaned past him to get her coat, Kenny felt her breast gouge into his shoulder, and she pressed a wad of crumpled paper into his palm. He quickly closed his fingers around it, and her lips brushed his ear.

"My address and 'phone," she whispered. "Just in case you change your mind about tonight. I hope so."

He tightened his hand in a small squeeze, because he felt it was expected of him, and then she had straightened up and was out of reach.

"Well, so long, girls," Mizoo grinned, patting Carol's buttocks just where they stretched the skirt to popping. She snapped erect in indignation. "Thanks for the party."

Carol jolted him with a savage slap on the cheek, and spinning on her heel, marched to the door.

"Merry Christmas, fellows," Clara said, and then she was gone into the crowd.

Ken and Mizoo sat in silence, sipping slowly from their glasses. Mizoo nursed the red glowing stain of Carol's hand lovingly.

"Well, that's that," he said. "I guess we stay bachelors tonight."

"It's probably just as well."

"Yeah. What the hell."

"Yeah, what the hell," Kenny's mind echoed, while his fist clenched around the crumpled paper in his hand, wondering what Clara might look like, nude, on a wide bed, in the dark, after he'd had a pint or so inside him.

MIDNIGHT:

I T HAPPENS, once every twenty-four hours, and is a split infinitive in time, an outcast thing; the witching hour, that vampires come to suck the blood; the time that the body can no longer fight death, resistance is low, and an old man, lying in crisp linen, on a four poster bed, surrounded by the best talent the AMA has to offer, with the heirs sipping coffee during their long last vigil, downstairs, and the old man opens his filmy eyes, showing a dead milky blue, in the last light of his life, and there is no more to see, he has seen it all, and he turns away, and deep down in what still remains alive of his brain. He is in tune with everything that lives with the great eye of God, as one last favor from the All-Being, for being forced to live a futile span of years, to perform his share of the hilarious experiment of life, and on this common ground that he so newly acquired, and is so shortly to lose, the desiccated old man can stand, as if on a mountain top, and look across through time and space, as though it were nothing—through the midnight, which is nothing—and see the other self of him and all the millions of other selfs, that would have been him, if he had followed another course than the one he took. He sees and envies, in that split second, that it is midnight, and he is lying dead in a back alley, surrounded by trash cans and littered bits of old bread and baked potato skins that have been thrown out by the cafe next door, the cats sniffing around his shoes, the muscatel bottle rolling from his hand, in the last spasm of death, and midnight is going, fleeting fast, and the two old men, who are really one old man, going with it—and the door is slammed and is never opened again, because who can really determine which moment is truly midnight, which tick of the clock is one day, and which is ticking on the next day, which is tomorrow, and when the rock is thrown into the lake, which instant does the stone cause the ripples or does the water ripple in anticipation of the stone, and how much time is consumed in the splash, how much space does each ripple occupy, and who knows these facts with true certainty. Only an All-Seeing and Omniscient God, who certainly regards the pitiful struggling microcosms on this clod of dirt, laughingly called Earth, and who being truly Omniscient, records that on midnight, Friday, December 24th or Saturday, December 25th, depending on how you view this tiny instant in time, such and such occurred. But for our purposes, yours and mine, all that actually interests us in that moment, is the people we know, or have passed through our field of ken, nodding, intent on their business, and as we listen, we can hear the report of the recording deity say that, in that suspended instant in time, Clara, heavy-headed, but clear-eyed, in the bright velvet air of the parking lot, unlocks her car and Carol stands behind her, hating her for being able to let down in the face of convention, while she, to whom all things are possible, finds it impossible to do the things she wants, and inside the building that they stand behind, Ken is echoing the words of Mizoo in his head. What the hell, what the hell, and they seem a slogan by which to govern his life, and Mizoo sits across from him and says these words, what the hell, but doesn't really feel them because he is thinking that Clara didn't need to call him ugly. He knew it, and if he could only have the face of Kenny, then he would show them all, but until he got those features, they would never know how they curdled his heart, when they called him names, and off on the other side of town, Beverly slept, curled into a ball, like a kitten, alone in a large bed, the alcohol vanishing, leaving her nothing but a nightmare of the old days in Memphis, and her Daddy coming to take her home, and in that instant, that is midnight, her legs shot straight in the bed, and she gave a moan and clutched at the pillow, as a piece of driftwood, to keep her afloat, and in another tiny room, in a small house, overlooking a lake, Bud lay beside a still form in the dark, with his hand cupping her breast, exhausted, but being driven into the rigors of passion again, and the girl turning to him, saying, "See, honey, you didn't need to get so mad. I was going to do it all the time, but you got me so drunky," and Connie, off in another direction, and the light too bright, it stuns you by contrast, bored, sitting across the table from Gladys, watching her and the fellow in the bright sport coat, making love, and the clever movement of the hands underneath the table, and wondering why she had come with Gladys, even as much as she needed someone, because with her it always turns out the same with Gladys, and though she denies that she is a push-over, she is pushed over nearly every time she steps from her front door, because she has the zest for living that can't bear to miss the most excruciating experiences life can offer, and then the instant is released from the pinch of the heavenly thumb, and the moment that is midnight is gone in a scrambling flash, scurrying to catch up to its true place in time, and the high school girl is huddled in the front seat of the car that belongs to her steady's father, and her steady's hand is under her skirt, and she is frightened, because it is the first time they have gone this far, and though she has heard that others have gone all the way, she doesn't want to tonight, because she is afraid, and her breath is coming fast and something deep inside that is the first stirrings of womanhood tells her to cling fast to the boy, and never let go, and to lie limp in his arms like a fertile field of wheat, awaiting the harvest, but she cannot, her fear is too great, and she kisses him quick on the nose, removing his hand from the elastic, running into the house away from him, shouting over her shoulder, "I've got to go, honey. Mother's waiting, and it's past midnight. Merry Christmas, darling."

SATURDAY, DECEMBER 25th ...
12:01 A.M.

"COME ON, honey. Your girl friend won't mind going home alone. Let me take you home. I'm a good kid."

"But I can't, Donnie. I came with Connie and I've got to go home with her."

Connie was sure they didn't know she was behind them, coming from the cigarette machine. She had finished an entire pack that night. They would have held their voices down, but the liquor had been flowing since Sport Coat had joined their table.

She'd had a few dances, but when she didn't respond to the line the wolves handed out, the men sought greener pastures. She didn't care. She was content to sit and think about Kenny and what a rotten situation she had made for herself. She had never been so lonely as she was, right this instant, and she envied Gladys her ability to let down and adapt herself to her surroundings.

Had Kenny been lonely? Was that why he had sought understanding elsewhere? She wondered if his pitch had been the time-worn "My wife just doesn't understand me" routine. She doubted it. No matter what you said about Kenny, he never used a corny line.

This Sport Coat character was loaded with the old ones.

She gave a ladylike cough so that she wouldn't catch the two off balance, though secretly, she was sick to death of watching Gladys succumb to the sorghum flattery that Donnie was manufacturing. She would rather believe fidelity of one of the six rowdies lined up at the bar she had just passed, than that slick haired smoothy, wrapped in color, that sat at her table. At least, those wolves were honest about their intentions, they didn't really expect to gratify their desires on the spot, it would have been a little awkward in a crowd, but anyway, they had let her know that they were agreeable to any proposition she might make.

"Hiya, honey. Where'd you get them lumps?"

"I've got an extra pillow upstairs I'm not using."

"Ooh what a machine. Zack, how'd you like to have that swing in your backyard?"

"I couldn't stand it without vitamin pills."

They had made her burn for a moment, until she realized they were really complimenting her in a left-handed manner. When you got around fellows like that, you'd have to sit tight, with your legs crossed, or they'd have you on the floor, in their exuberance, for life. Anyway you knew at least where you stood, at all times, because they were honest in their desires, and not slinking behind your back with those cloying little flatteries that was not flattery at all, but insults to your intelligence and perception. All men were the same, rutting dogs around a bitch in heat. Yield an inch, and they would come swarming around your carefully constructed barriers, like fat yellow maggots.

There was honesty in surrendering yourself, knowing that your partner considered you in the same biological light that you regarded him, each having different attachments, necessary ones to complete the function you were intended for. To view the situation objectively, deciding coldly that you each had use for the other for an hour or so, and when the time was up, with no reservations or commitments, rising and bidding each other good-bye. Without any tearful clinging and last minute disillusionment, as so often happens.

"You want another drink?" Donnie asked her.

"I've still got part of the last one left."

"You might as well lay in a supply. It's going to be a long winter."

She didn't want to drink Donnie's liquor, but if he was silly enough to throw it around, why should she pass it up. Besides, this was all part of this phony build-up he was giving Gladys, and she might as well make the set-up as expensive for him as she could.

"Where's the waitress?" he asked, swiveling his head from one side to the other, so that Connie saw the line of dirt around the collar of his shirt. "I'd better get them at the bar."

"Isn't he a cute fellow, Connie?" Gladys said, when he had left them. "I like him."

"So it seems. I guess he's all right. He just isn't my type."

"The world would be in bad shape if we all went after the same fellow."

"I guess so."

"He wants to take me home," Gladys said, simply, throwing her line into the pool.

"Well?"

"He's a nice guy, and the air's so warm and beautiful tonight. I'd really like to go."

"What's holding you back? Fear?"

For a moment, Gladys was puzzled.

"What is there to be afraid of?"

"Nothing. What I meant was, if you want to go with Donnie, why don't you go?"

"But I have my car here, and besides, I came with you. I can't run out on you."

"Don't worry about me. I can sit and cry into my drinks alone. Just give me the key to your car, and I'll take it home and bring it to your house tomorrow."

"Oh, I couldn't do that." Gladys' eyes were wide. "It wouldn't be fair to you."

"Don't be silly. What difference does it make to me? You go ahead. I'll be all right. It will be some of my Christmas present to you."

"Thanks, honey. I'll take you up on it." Gladys sighed with relief.

When Donnie came back, Gladys said, "Connie here, is going to take my car home later. She's going to help them close this place. Going to try to drink all the whiskey they have in the place.

"Shall we leave, when we finish these drinks, Gladys?" he asked after a few moments.

"Okay."

After Gladys had led her trophy in triumph from the room, and after two or three solitary drinks, Connie started for the lounge. When she passed the bar, she felt a hand on her arm. Before she stopped and turned to face him, she knew it was one of the six who had sat at the bar earlier in the evening. The one who hadn't commented on her passing before, but had sat, sullenly staring into his drink. The other five had gone.

She turned slowly to face him, his clear, dark eyes boring into hers, with a hint of pain and a little promise. Her eyebrows lifted.

"Care to dance?" he asked, and his voice was low and throaty, causing a nerve spasm to travel the stairway of her spine.

She nodded.

"Wait until I put my bag on the table."

"I'll go with you."

"All right. It will only take a second."

As they walked onto the floor, she turned to face him, and his arm went around her like a steel rod, tight and hard. He held her close, as though he would never release her.

He was quite tall, without that gangling stoop that afflicted so many tall men; but he was more substance than shadow, deep in the chest, hard and flat in the stomach. His face was darkly tan, under blue-black, curling hair. He had surprising light blue eyes, like twin beacons shining out of the darkness. It was apparent that his clothes were tailor made, because no forty-nine dollar suit, with an extra pair of pants thrown in on easy budget terms, could achieve that air of studied carelessness that was embodied in the skillful sweep of the coat. His snowy, white shirt was as full as velvet, and the tie that adorned it was colorful, yet discreet, studded with a gold bauble of some sort. He wore matching cuff links.

There was just a suggestion of a hollow under each cheek, as though he were suffering from malnutrition, but Connie knew that this wasn't the case. You see this groove under the cheekbone of many Westerners, bleached by the sun, skin tightening hard around the eyes from squinting into the glare of bright weather. He might be part Indian, she thought. He looks dark enough.

There were few people left on the floor, and for several minutes, they did not speak. Her hair lay against his face, and their bodies were in tune with each other. They danced faultlessly.

He spoke first.

"Your friends go off and leave you?"

The contentment she felt was such that she hated to break it.

"Mmm-mmmm. Yours?"

"Boys were all tired out. Had a long trip."

"Yes? Where are you from?"

"We're all Texas boys, Miss. Come in from Dallas."

"Do you have friends you visit here for Christmas?"

"No'm, we're just having us a vacation. I've known 'em all my life and they work in my father's oil field."

"So you brought them out here for a vacation?"

"Well, it's partly business for me. I got to see about buyin' some more drillin' rigs."

"How do you like California?"

"I been out here before. But, I'll take Dallas any time. We got all your weather and no smog. And it ain't as crowded. We got lots of room to move around in."

"That's because you haven't got the people wanting to come there and live, like we have."

"Now, let's not argue about states, before we even know each other, Miss. I don't even know your name yet, and you're sayin' somethin' that people get shot or tarred and feathered for, back home."

"Connie. Connie Lawrence. Native daughter of the Golden State."

"Cash Hardin. Third generation under Sam Houston."

The music had stopped and they were on their way back to Connie's table. She reached across and shook his hand.

"Put her there, pardner."

"You bet, Connie." He grasped her hand strongly.

Connie felt in that touch a certain kinship, apart from the meeting of two members of the opposite sex. It was not the feeling of irresistible attraction, stemming out of a physical need, but rather, a comradeship for another member of the human race.

"How about the next dance, Connie?"

"All right, Cash," she said, and their eyes met, and she felt a faint stirring inside herself, as though something heavy had been moved from one side of her to the other.

As he shifted from one foot to the other, in a moment's hesitation, before he turned to go back to the bar to wait for the music, she stopped him.

"Don't go," she said, touching his elbow. "Stay and talk 'til the set begins. We'll be dancing again, in a minute."

He looked into her eyes, and they were dark and wide and shining.

"I'll get my drink and be right back," he said, and she watched the broad shoulders, tapering into a slim, hipless waist, stride off across the floor. Ken, or no Ken, it was a breathless, dare and double dare feeling to think that you had started a juggernaut of emotions in action, that you might not be able to control later. She had invited him to sit with her. To some people, this might be as good as a proposition to spend the night. She wondered how Cash would take it. He seemed like a nice guy, but you could never tell by appearances. Well, he knew where he stood now, and if he knew the angles, he'd know he had a clear track ahead.

She had asked him to sit down; he knew that she was at loose ends this evening, had no one to look out for her. This might grow into a Frankenstein of unleashed passion, that no one could stop.

Why should they control it, she asked herself. Had Kenny ever shown the slightest desire to master his impulses, on any occasion? She remembered that, at one time, that was one of the reasons she had succumbed to his advances, when they had had a spat and she wasn't going to let him touch her. She was all keyed up and she had laid, huddled in a ball, with her back to him, mute, unfeeling, and his desire seemed uncontrollable, and finally, rather than fight him, she had turned and allowed herself to drown in the fire of his passion.

But that was gone now, and she had to build a new life. A new house to live in. Kenny was a state of mind, a habit pattern that she must break. And the quickest way was the cleanest way, after all.

Cash had come back. He laid his hand on her arm. She smiled at him, sitting across from her, as she struggled out of her revery.

"Changed your mind about me?" he asked, his dark brows drawing down into a frown.

"Oh, no. Just dreaming, I guess."

"What's the matter?" Cash asked, leaning toward her another fraction of an inch. "Somebody giving you trouble?"

"There isn't anything the matter," she lied. "It's nothing ... there's nothing anybody can do."

His hand slowly caressed her arm, traveling down to her fingertips. He toyed with her rings, pushing them up to her knuckle, and then back to the groove in the flesh that had been worn by four years of constant wearing. In a flash of perception, like a radar signal transmitted from his fingertips through her bones, she knew what he was about to say, before his lips parted.

"Your old man giving you trouble?"

"Kind of," she nodded, her eyes still on the table.

"God, I'm a nosy rascal, aren't I? I'll shut up and go away, if you want to be alone with it."

"No, Cash. Stay here and talk. I'm alone enough now."

"Something bright and witty? I'm afraid I can't oblige. I never was a fancy one with words."

"It doesn't have to be fancy. Just ordinary and something to brush away this dream I've been living in for the last four years."

His fingers tightened on her arm again.

"You are having a hard time of it, aren't you, Connie girl?"

"These things happen in the best of regulated families. I don't want to bore you with my troubles."

"But I want to make your troubles my troubles, too."

Connie raised her eyes and smiled at him. Her dark hair framed her face, as she said seriously, "No, they're not important enough to load on your shoulders, although you're very sweet to volunteer. Let's drink up and have another. Live a little, tomorrow may be too late. Let's have our Christmas party right now."

Cash smiled at her, still holding on to her hand. She felt a strange kinship with him. They were both so alone. He, because he was so far from home on this Christmas Eve, and she, because she had elected to be alone. She had chosen to shut herself off from the world she had known, the world that had taken her hopes, ideals and dreams, and had ground them in the dust. She was in training for the delights of promiscuous flesh, rather than domestic flesh, and Cash was her first real contact with that other world.

She squeezed his hand in response.

"What would you like to do first, little one?" he asked.

"Are you with me in this party project?"

"Every step of the way."

"What time is it?"

"Ten of one."

"How about, let's have some food, and a couple more drinks."

"Sound idea."

"Where shall we go to eat?" she asked, lighting a cigarette, from the pack he had lying on the table.

"What's the matter with here?"

"Can you eat here this late?"

"Anything your little heart desires."

"Steak and onions?" Connie told herself that as long as she was in the game, she might as well play it out to the last card.

"If that's what you want."

"Order it. I'll bet you won't."

"What'll you bet? A kiss?" he asked, zeroing her in with his eyes.

Those eyes, she decided, would be her downfall. They were so piercing, that when she looked in them, they fastened her down, and she couldn't look away, until his glance shifted. They seemed able to peer into the inner recesses of her being, and when they pleaded with her, as now, how could she refuse?

"If you like," she said, slowly.

There was a flash of triumph in his voice, as he shouted for the waiter, and his eyes possessed her for a moment, as the man left with their order. She felt the heat of his gaze, as she raised her glass and drank, and she felt the flush of warming blood mounting to her cheeks.

This was a thing to consider. If he could look at her in this way and cause the blood to charge through her veins, there must surely be something, an invisible bond, an unseen golden chain, binding them together. Surely his glance and stare told her that she meant more to him, in just this last half-hour, than she had ever meant to Kenny, in all the four years they had been married. If Cash wanted her, and needed her, on this Christmas morning, why shouldn't she go to him? She would get a certain strength and a sense of dependence from him, in return for the things that she would give.

She laughed, over the rim of her glass, and he echoed it, and clinked the glass with his.

He. was pensive and moody, while they ate. His face clouded like a thunderhead blowing across the valley, casting a dark shadow before it, along the desert floor.

Connie sensed the change in his manner.

"What's your problem, Cash? You think buying me a meal was a bad investment?"

A smile flickered across his face and was gone.

"No, no. Nothing like that. I was just thinking about something that was none of my business. How I could help you out. Maybe I could, if you'd let me."

"I think you're sweet to think about me, but it's just husband trouble, and something that no one can help me with. Something I've got to work out myself."

"What is it? Does your husband chase around, and expect you to be waiting when he gets home?"

Connie waited until she had let the smoke coast out of her lungs.

"No, it's not that exactly. I go out a lot too. Not to bars, like tonight. But to meetings and other social activities, and he figures that because I've got a busy life, he can fool around with every floozy in town."

"That's the trouble with a lot of guys. They get one woman, and when the thrill of conquest is gone, it's all over. The little woman is just another girl now, they had all that she has to offer, and they want to see what it's like in somebody else's back yard."

She nodded her head slowly, like the last tolling of a funeral bell. She was feeling deliciously sorry for herself now.

"That might be true. I never thought I was too much of a bargain, but at least, if I'm married to the guy, I should be able to expect a little consideration."

Cash squeezed her hand again. "Well, I don't know how you feel about it, but I know what I'd do, if it were me."

"What's that?"

"Serve him what he dishes out. He evidently has been mighty high-handed in what he does, and what he figures you will take. Find out just how much of it he can take."

This was it. The fork in the road. She could go in any direction she wanted. She could stand up and say, "No, he'll come around. I'll just go home and wait." But why should she be so pathetically noble? She'd already tried that, and what had it gotten her? A kick in the teeth. She had set out tonight to be a hellion, a real, slinky siren, and up to now, she'd done nothing but sip weak drinks, dance a couple of times, and watch Gladys being led up the garden path.

Now was the time to hold her breath and take the plunge.

"Why do you think I'm here all alone?" she said, looking down at the table, seemingly blasé, but with nerve ends tingling and a certain tight squeezing in the stomach. "Why do you think I asked you to sit with me?"

There was a moment's silence, as Cash digested that last revelation.

"I always stop at this hotel, when I'm in the Los Angeles area," Cash said.

"Are you in town often?" she asked, with outward serenity, but inwardly feeling herself swelling with excitement.

"Once or twice a year," he answered. "But I don't have a car with me. We flew out."

"What difference does it make about a car?"

"Well, this place closes pretty soon. Unless you'd like to come up to the room for a drink?"

"All right, Cash. But don't get the wrong idea. This is for fun and games tonight. To lose myself, maybe, lose a little bitterness."

"That means you're coming up?"

"Yes, Cash. I'm coming up."

"Well, what are we waiting for? Let's finish this meal and get the show on the road."

And the thing that grew between them, compounded itself in silence. They bent over their food, and each could feel the power of the other's personality, glowing strong, like a hurricane lamp in the storm, and their imaginations painted glittering pictures of the love and devotion they would find together. They would seek new heights of passion never before known to mortal man or woman.

At least, Connie's imagination told her all this. She couldn't be sure of the trend of Cash's mind. At times, he had an almost calculating expression on his face. It would be a blow to her pride, if nothing else, if she were to learn that she was no more than a new experience to him.

But, no, that couldn't be. He was too sincere. They understood each other. A meeting of the minds on some unknown telepathic plane, gently rubbing thought together, and passing on into opposite directions.

That would be the way of it, she told herself. They would never hold to each other longer than tonight. In the morning, he would be gone forever, but at least, she had found a common meeting ground with someone, other than her husband, and it gave her a momentary confidence that she could still be desired by another man.

It might give her a firm basis for her future actions. If she were still desirable, as she had secretly known all the time, she wouldn't be as lonely without Ken. Only her heart would still be all alone.

And no matter how nice Cash would seem, how tender he would try to be, he'd still not be Ken, whose every touch, technique and caress, was engraved from memory on her very being. He would be an adulterated substitute, but she would never let him know. It wasn't his fault, poor darling.

Suddenly, she felt his hand holding hers tighter, drawing her across the table, forcing her to lean toward him. She tried to draw away for a moment, but it was futile to fight his strength, and she waited until his lips were moistly grazing hers, and then she turned her head swiftly. His mouth buried in her ear, and he pulled her in still closer. She could feel his breath, as though it were a molten physical thing, and it caused a tremble to go through her body.

"Not here," she breathed. "Not here. This isn't the place."

"I know, I know. But when I look at you, I can't wait. I've got to have you soon, or I'll bust."

"Patience, patience. Don't get lost."

"I'll never find my way back now."

"Oh yes you will. You're a long way from being lost."

"Don't try to test my will power right now."

"What do you mean?"

"Just don't come too close, that's all."

"Why? What would you do if I did?"

"Damn you, but you're a temptress. Why do you kid me so, when you don't really mean it?"

This time, Connie leaned forward, voluntarily, brushing his cheek with a slow, sultry kiss, feeling her breast pulse against his hand.

"Who says I don't really mean it? Show me the man that said it."

"Here he is," Cash laughed, pointing to himself. "I'm the guy. I said it."

"Can you prove that?"

"I want to prove that I'm wrong. I want to prove you do care."

"How are you going to do it?"

"By making love to you, honey, so that you'll forget all about the man you left at home. So that the only one you'll be able to think about is me, Cash Hardin."

"What makes you think I'm thinking about him now? Don't worry about him. He's not home. He's out having a big time for himself."

"Prove to me that you're not thinking about him. Kiss me. Now. Hard," he commanded.

She hesitated a moment, then reaching slowly across the table, she ran her fingers into his hair, until she had a handful. She rose, and bent to him, pulling his face up to hers, by the hair, and fastening her ripe, carmined lips on his, half-parted, and moist with unconcealed longing. She held him, until she could feel the breath of him gusting between his teeth and between hers. She had a sense of exhilaration, until his fingers, like vise-like hooks, began digging into her arms, and her muscles ached cruelly, under the pressure of them.

It was he who broke finally.

"Let's get out of here," he cried, looking wildly about him for the waiter.

"What's your hurry?" She was smiling now, her eyes half-closed.

"Don't be foolish. You can't fool around dynamite with a blow torch, that's all."

She gave him the Mona Lisa again.

"So?" It was fun to play with them, like cat and mouse. That was the way it had been with Kenny. She could drive him nearly out of his mind by teasing.

He tried to help her with her coat, but somehow, they couldn't manage it between them, so she put it over her arm, and after he had paid and tipped the waiter, not enough, judging from the scowl he wore, they went out of the little bar, filled with green leather booths, and down a long wide hall, into a grand lobby, that could be converted into a train terminal, with little or no alteration. Past the sportily clad night clerk, dozing over his magazine, for something more alert, with a raucous, unintelligible voice, dressed in shiny serge, with a peak cap, and across the deep piled rug, to the bank of elevators.

They could see by the lights above, that only one was working, and it was shuttling people around in the upper intestines of the hotel. Cash and Connie stood in the glare of the impersonal light of the lobby, nuzzling each other, like colts in a field, and waited. Finally, sure enough, the doors swung wide and a grinning face beckoned them inside.

"Evenin' Mist' Cash," the operator said. "This yo' new wife tonight?"

"Don't get your water hot, Sam. It's a wife. What's the difference whether she's new or not."

"Sure, Mist' Cash. What I care who you brings up in this car? Am I the house cop?"

"Your eyes bug out enough, and your feet're flatter'n a snake's navel."

"Sho,' sho,' Mist' Cash. You sho' a caution."

Connie felt as though she would like to fold into herself, until there was nothing of her to be seen, but a little bundle of old clothes on the floor, and she might as well be, for the way that Negro and Cash talked about her. Like she was a common prostitute.

Then the other side of her mind took control. Shouted her virtuous conscience into oblivion.

What the hell was she, if she wasn't a damn, common prostitute? Here she was going up to a strange room with a man that she had only met an hour or so before. He had led her into sweet surrender, just by buying her a three-dollar steak dinner. Even the common run of the mill prostitute sold out for more than that. What had this latest scrap with Kenny started? She had really come down tonight. Just about as far as you could get.

And how could she back out now? And besides that, Cash was getting funnier every minute. There was something sneaky about his eyes, a squint or a glance that she didn't like.

But here she was, and she might as well make the best of it.

And then they were out of the elevator, Cash, holding her elbow tightly, steering her with an eager force, down the long, bleak hall, that stretched into musty eternity. She felt a clawing, frightening nausea in her throat, and she felt she must turn and run back to the grinning Negro that stood gawking from the elevator, and implore him to take her back to the lobby again. Where she could run into the night, and home to Kenny again. But that was silly and unthinkable, because, for one thing, she didn't have Kenny any more, and she was supposed to be a woman of the world, or, at least, that was the impression she had tried to give Cash, and her pride wouldn't let her back out now.

And then, suddenly, her skies were clear again, the sudden panic gone like a summer storm, and as she turned and looked up at him, he had a serene smile on his face, and he bent his head and kissed her again, pressing the key to his apartment into her hand.

"Go ahead, Connie, you open the door. If you really want to. I don't want you to feel that I'm trying to force you into anything."

"I came up here, because I wanted to." She smiled back. "For a drink, because you said you have some in the icebox."

"Let's face facts. I brought you, because I want to make love to you, you gorgeous brunette. Mad, mean love."

"How mad? How mean?" she asked, provocatively.

They were standing before the door, and at her words, he turned suddenly, like a striking snake, and gathered her into his arms, smashing her lips against his, and she could feel the deep strength of his chest, as he pulled her in to him, and her breast pulsed tightly against his body, and their lips clung and were bruised by the impact. The fibres in the muscles of her arms and the ligaments and tendons of her calves and thighs, ran down into water, and she clung to him to keep from falling to the floor. Her body, soul and being, were rushing to that one point of their connection, and she couldn't open her eyes, they were sealed in ecstasy, and finally, when it seemed she was going down for the third time, he released her and stepped away. She reached out for the door jamb, as she wavered for a second.

"Will that do for a start?"

She nodded, mutely.

"I need you, darling. I've been thinking about nothing else all evening, even though I do think I hid it pretty well."

"That's why I came up." She sighed. "I needed someone too, I guess."

"Where's the key? Let's get inside and have a drink and settle down to the business at hand."

But the key was on the floor, and they had to scramble for a moment, before Cash came up with it.

Connie laughed, helping him up from the floor.

"Your kisses are too potent. That last one was a paralyzer."

"If I'd had the key, it would have melted in my hand."

She took the key from him, and his lips were in her hair, and brushing her ear, as she unlocked the door. He stepped past her and flicked on the lights, catching her for another kiss as she came into the apartment.

"Here, darling," he said, laying his cigarettes on a low coffee table, done in blonde oak, to match the other furniture in the room, "give us your coat, and I'll lay it on the bed. I'll bring the drinks back with me."

When he left the room, Connie looked around her, gazing in awe at the luxury of the apartment. She sat on one-half of a large, coral sectional lounge, each side of which was as large as her own overstuffed couch at home. Dusky green drapes hid the windows, which were large and covered all of one wall of the room. Fine oil paintings relieved the walls; deep piled, dove gray rugs on the floors. One of those seven-inch television sets sat in one corner. Cash probably paid as much rent in a week, on this apartment, as she and Kenny gave the bank, for their monthly house payment.

"Do you like this place, honey?" Cash was back, with a glass in each hand.

"Oh, yes. It's lovely."

"It's not as nice as home, but it will do until I get back."

"I spent so much time staring at this room, and the lovely things in it, that I forgot all about our cigarettes."

"Never mind, I'll get 'em. Have a snort of this," Cash said, handing her the glass. "It'll make hair grow."

"I've got plenty."

"You have, at that." His eyelids were heavy as he stared at her, and she could feel the warmth of his eyes boring into the very inside of her being, and the blood began to course in her veins with such force, that she could nearly feel it surging from one end of her body to the other, with the fierce tread of a caged beast.

He sat beside her on the couch, and for a long moment, neither said a word. Then he turned and got a cigarette in silence, and she could see in the soft light, that his fingers trembled ever so slightly. She felt the delicious quivering of her own nerves, a slow tightness in her limbs, that was like the quiet turning of a spring that must keep getting ever tighter, until the strength of the metal is gone, and it can take no more and finally snaps. And in that moment of snapping, the damage is done.

Connie sipped the drink he had handed her, until the cigarette was placed in her hand. Then she had a puff or two, like an automaton, and he sat beside her quietly. Their common meeting ground had vanished, and the reason they were in the room together, stood stark in front of them, and faced them, and they could do nothing to refute its silent accusations. So they peered into their glasses, until they had finished their drink, and Cash went in and brought another.

But before they could touch it, Connie reached across and put her hand on his arm to stop him. She felt cold, alone and shut out of his thoughts. She wanted to stop the deadly silence that was withering the evening. He mistook her meaning, and gathered her into his arms again. Their lips surged together, and the longing that had been put aside for those few minutes, came back to take possession with even greater force. She surrendered her mouth and her breath in one passionate gust of emotion, and she could feel him crush her even tighter, in the strong confidence of conquest. She knew that there were some proprieties to observe, some things she must stop him from doing, until just a little later, but her resolutions were weak. It couldn't happen right there, between them, as though they were a pair of wild beasts of the field, that had never known order or restraint, but her thoughts were so confused that his hand was starting to climb past her knee, before she pulled it away without removing her lips from his, but it really did no good, because, in another minute, he was right back. But she could be strong too, and she jerked his hand away just as it reached the top of her nylons and shook her head violently, under the pressure of his lips, and he stopped for a minute or two.

Then they broke apart, and took a sip of their drinks, without saying a word, just looking deep into each other's eyes, as though they were trying to hypnotize each other. Her cigarette did nothing to erase the passion he had stirred in her veins. The smoke was as hot to her tissues, as was his touch. When she had exhaled the smoke, he gathered her back into his arms as simply as he had released her, and fastened her to him in another breath-taking kiss.

Her arms crept up around his back, as though they had a will of their own. Her fingers found his crisp, curling hair, and coiled and sported luxuriously in the rings of it. And all the blood in her body seemed rushing to her head, and there was a flaming, roaring around her ears, and her nerves seemed to shrivel and shrink and pull in, and she had to pull Cash in closer, her arms straining at his back.

It was not that this sensation was new to her. It was and it wasn't. The same basic sensations occurred each time she faced glorious submission, such as this. It was curious that no matter what happened to her body and her weakening will, one part of her mind could remain detached, and view the entire scene from about six feet away. But this time, there was a new element added.

It was someone else. And while much of the descent into passion was made by the same path, there were some turns and short cuts that were new and different, because of the new guide conducting her tour.

And then suddenly, as she opened her eyes, she attempted to compose herself by another sip of her drink, and another puff on his cigarette. After the next kiss, time and reality seemed to go swirling away from her like something caught up in the suck of a vacuum cleaner. She went under and Cash had his hand up under her dress, doing something that just made her worse, and then, he had the upper part unbuttoned, and her breasts were in his hands, and she couldn't bring herself to try to make him stop, and once, she squirmed and kicked her glass over on the rug, as he bent his mouth to her breast and bit her, and then it was all right because he was kissing the part he had bit, and she was kissing him with everything she had. And then, all the buttons were loose.

The lights were out.

He came back to the couch in the dark. Kicking the coffee table.

She could feel the harsh tweed of his sleeves against her bare skin, as he leaned down, picking her up in his arms.

She buried her face in his neck, and she held him tight, as he carried her across the room.

She could feel the vibrations in his skin, between her teeth, as he murmured love things to her in the dark.

And he was heavy, and they went off into a world of their own for a minute or two.

Then it was over.

It was contentment, warmth and goodness, and she dozed.

He struck a match to light a cigarette.

Now he had to think of his friends in the room next door.

2:16 A.M.

"JEEZ, there's not a hell of a lot left." Mizoo rocked the bottle back and forth to gauge the level, raised it against the windshield of Kenny's Ford, and peered through it toward the glare of the street lamp, a half block down the shaded street on which they were parked. The glass glinted dully and Ken could see from where he sat that there wouldn't be more than two or three drinks apiece left.

Mizoo raised it to his lips.

"Careful," Ken cautioned, "it's too late to get any more."

"Don't worry. I'll save you some."

Ken didn't really want any more to drink. It was bubbling out of his ears now. He could feel the blind rage of the alcohol behind his eyes now, burning to get out, searing all his senses, making them dull and wooden. His mouth and tongue felt numb. But, what the hell, he told himself. Mizoo was a good guy. Why should he refuse to drink Mizoo's whiskey, forgetting for the moment, that he was the one who had made the purchase. And he was a good guy and so was Mizoo and they had been sitting there, killing this pint for nearly two hours, so why not have another one, even if he felt a little sick.

"Merry Christmas," Ken said, "And up yours, too."

"Happy New Year," Mizoo answered. "And up yours double."

Ken took another swallow out of the bottle, because he had just remembered who bought it.

"So what were you so hot on telling me, when you got thirsty all of a sudden?" he asked, when he had finished drinking and had handed the bottle back to Mizoo.

"I was talking about my first wife, when I got out of the Navy. You was askin' how come I come to California. It was because of my first wife."

"What about her? And hurry up with that bottle."

"She was the cause of all my troubles."

"Women always are. God, I oughta tell you about mine. My wife and my troubles."

"Well, I'd known this girl in Bloomfield, almost all my life, I guess. I was a farm boy, lived on the farm about eight miles out of town, and had to come on the bus to go to school and all of that. The city kids always got snooty with us farm kids, even though my pop had one of the biggest farms in the county, and it didn't seem to make no difference to those city kids, even though maybe their pop worked in a gas station and they never got no more to eat than side meat and grits. Belle was one of them kids, and I should've known better than to get mixed up with her in the first place. But she was a looker, built like a brick house, with the upstairs balconies all in place. Long, yellow hair and legs to make your mouth water, even if you was a family man. Met her on a hay ride us farm boys had one night, she was with some other guy, and he got all drunk up, and I was drivin' or somethin'. Anyway, I didn't have no girl, and she come up on the old buckboard with me, and she was lovin' me up, while I had hold of the reins. Damnedest thing you ever saw."

"You get into her?"

"Not that night. I think she was queer or somethin'. But anyway, she did what she could, with me holdin' the reins and all. But later, I went down to her house in town, and her folks and her brother all went out to a show, and she took me right into her momma and daddy's room, and we laid right on the bed, right on the spread, and did it, and just got everything straightened out when her folks come in."

"I'll bet that scared you good."

"It was a near one, all right, but that didn't stop us. No, sir. She was the hottest little devil I ever see, and that sort of thing should of tipped me off, that if she'd do it to a farm boy that easy, just like that, how would she be around a city kid? But I didn't care, 'cause I was just a nineteen-year-old punk, and Belle was seventeen then, I reckon. Yeah, she must have been seventeen, and it was the first steady stuff I'd ever had, and I was crazy with it, like a hound dog. So it was ever' Friday night on her mommy's bed, because we didn't hold back a minute, but handled the whole damned thing like the silly ass kids we were, and then, one night, her folks had seen the second feature."

"Holy Christ! What happened then? Did they catch you in the act?"

"Right smack in the middle. The bedroom door opened right into the front room, and we'd gotten so damn careless, that we'd gone right into the bedroom, leavin' all the lights on, and the door open, and when her folks opened the front door of the house, all they had to do was look."

"What did you do?"

"Belle and I scrambled for some clothes, but it didn't do much good. There was some real fur flyin' and her daddy hit me a clop, but he was littler than me, and he only tried that once. After he got up off the floor, and Belle was cryin' and ever-thing, the three of them flustered me into sayin' I'd marry her."

"That was okay, wasn't it? You were in love with her, weren't you?"

"That's the thing. I loved her while I thought I was sneakin' somethin' over on ever'body. The thrill of doin' it on her daddy's nice clean bed. But when it got all over town, and I had to marry her, and I found out I wasn't the only one who was sneakin' it from her, in one place or another, it was a different story. And, anyway, my people weren't happy about the whole thing."

"You went ahead and married her anyway?"

"Had to. I was only nineteen, like I said, and farm kids are still pretty green at nineteen. I took her out to the farm, but she didn't like being away from the city and was always beggin' me to take her into a dance or a show, after I had been on slavin' my ass off to keep her in grub all day long. Finally she got so fed up with the farm, that she run away one afternoon and went back to her daddy's place. When I went in to get her, she wouldn't come away, and finally, I had to work in her daddy's gas station and live at her folk's house with her, but we never did do it on her daddy's bed again."

"Did you bring her to California with you?"

"Nope. She never lasted that long. Her daddy went under, and I was out of a job, and nobody in town would hire a farm boy, and they all knew what I was the one that got hooked into marryin' Belle, so one day, I decided I was through and went down to St. Louis and joined the Navy."

Kenny thought that was the end of it, and had another swallow from the bottle, handing it back to Mizoo, who drank and went on.

"I guess I was just fed up with seein' Belle around, so I went to sea, and more or less, forgot about her. When I got back to Bloomfield, she was gone. Last I heard, she was workin' as a call girl in Indianapolis."

"You said you came to California because of what your first wife did to you," Ken said. "What did she do to make you come out here?"

"Do you think I could stay in Bloomfield, with ever'body in town knowin' she was a whore up in Indiana? What would you do if your wife turned into a whore?"

"Probably the same thing. Head out."

Mizoo nodded. He drained the last drop out of the bottle, then rolled the car window down, and pitched the bottle into the street. The night quiet was split around them in a shattering crash.

Somewhere behind the trees, a gruff dog started to bark. The windows in the house in front of which they were parked, began to shine with light.

Ken turned the key in the ignition, kicking the engine into life.

"Christ, that's done it. We'd better shag ass."

"It's been a washout, hasn't it," said Mizoo.

"Hell. Let's go home and forget about tonight."

Ken turned into a main street of some kind, with a double set of car tracks running in the middle, but it was completely deserted, and their tiny car seemed to crawl the length of it as though it were being drawn along on a string.

They drove in silence, under the spell of the intense desolation surrounding them. The compact quiet through which they traveled seemed to close in around them, stifling, strangling, shutting them away from the real world, condemning them to travel lonely back streets for the rest of their lives.

Mizoo shuddered and reached into Kenny's upper pocket for a cigarette.

"Here's my street. Next one to the left."

"Okay," Kenny said, as he made the curve. "I've got to pick up my suit."

"You can keep those things you've got on, to drive home. Drop them by some day."

"I will. And I've got to take it slow going home. If the law ever grabs me with the load I've got on ... "

"You'll be all through drivin' for a while."

"Damn right."

After Mizoo had gone in for his clothes, and he had them safely in the seat beside him, Ken drove slowly into the deserted boulevard again, and started toward home. A paralyzing lethargy stole over him and the world seemed in slow motion. The morning air was warm and softly caressing, like warm oil on his skin, and he felt it was a damn shame they couldn't have lined up a couple women tonight. He would like to be in bed right now. Connie was out, God knew where, and he would give his blood in a silver bucket, if he could be with her. But after what had happened, that was hardly likely.

A vision of Beverly rose in front of his eyes. They were sandy and hard to focus, but he could see her as a vision of loveliness, not with her impossible glasses, or her whining sickness, the way she had been at the end, but the way it started.

Her lips on his, in the motor court, as she undressed and came to him, and some of the things she did, and the way she played with him to get him started. He knew he was nuts to think of those things now, it wouldn't do him any good. He couldn't do anything about it. He'd be lucky if Connie would let him into the house, when he got home, let alone, into the same bed with her. But he was a man, and he didn't have to take this torment, if he could think of some other way.

It was when he reached into his pocket for another cigarette, that he found the scrap of paper that gave him the way out. In the glow of an overhead street lamp, he found Clara's phone number.

He couldn't get shot for trying. He'd pull into the next all night gas station.

She was big and hefty, if he remembered right, but she had plenty on her bones, and what the hell, any port in a storm. She was probably in bed, it had been a couple hours or more, since she had left the joint. But there was just a chance, if she had meant what she said.

The lights gleamed ahead on the left, and he pulled in, back of the station, near the lube rack. A green kiosk stood at the back of the lot. He had a rough time getting over to it, once he was on his feet. The combination of the air and the exertion required to make the trip, made him dizzy and he had to sit on the tiny seat, inside the booth, before he could fish the nickel out of his trouser pocket. Then it was in the slot, and he was dialing.

He could hear the dull grinding of the bell, far on the other side of the line, and he held his breath in anticipation, and just a little fear seeped chilling through his bones, as he thought of the thing he was doing. Calling someone he didn't even know, at this ungodly hour.

"Yes?" A voice way off there.

"Clara?"

"Yes." A rising inflection, puzzled.

"Guess who this is."

"I know," she said, and her voice was getting clearer, as though she was waking up.

"Who then?"

"I don't remember your name. You're the blond fellow in the bar."

"That's right. Kenny."

"What are you doing up? How come you're not in bed? It's after two-thirty in the morning."

"I know. Merry Christmas, Clara."

"You're nuts. Merry Christmas."

"Still ready for some fun and games?" Ken asked.

"You sound high as a kite. You're probably ready for bed."

"That's the idea. Still want to add me to your collection?"

"Well, I've been asleep ... "

"You got anything to drink in the icebox?"

"Just a couple quarts of beer."

"That's better than nothing."

"You want some beer?"

"That's not all I want."

"We'll see about the other, when you get here. See what kind of shape you're in."

"Just try me. How do I get out to your place?"

He listened to the bearings she gave him, and after he had confirmed his route by checking it with the night man in the station, an old fellow, with a walrus mustache and no teeth, he headed out into the night again.

It was a large house, screened with rank shrubbery, and he could almost taste the scent of the flowers that grew along the walk, as he went up the door. He leaned against the jamb and rang the bell.

There wasn't a light to be seen in this part of the house, and he thought that perhaps she had given him the wrong directions, just to get rid of him, but no, the door opened and she loomed there in the dark. She took his arm and guided him inside.

He turned to face her, and to get the whole thing off on the right foot, he gathered her into his arm and pulled her in tight, kissing her, and he could taste the moist lips and the beer that she had tasted since he had called. She was large in his embrace, and he could feel that she had nothing on but a light housecoat, but her flesh felt firm underneath. He grasped her still tighter, and his hands slipped under the wrap, where it was loosely pulled together, and he had his hand cupping her breast. It was smooth and cool there, in the dark, but its muscular fiber was loose, and it did not resist the pressure of his hand.

Her mouth bored into his, and he felt her breath on his face, and he had the sudden shocking feeling that he was kissing his mother, and the thoughts that coursed his mind shook him, and he stiffened momentarily. Then, another part of him came to the fore, scourging the thought of his mother. He concentrated on the kiss.

It was long, but when their lips parted, she still refused to release him, but held him close in the dark of the large room, which smelled of old wood paneling, musty, overstuffed furniture and rubber plants. It was strange, foreign, and he felt completely out of it, but now that he had come this far, he couldn't very well back out of it.

She left him now, standing alone in the stifling silence, and he could hear her padding across the room. He wished that he was somewhere else, and at the same time, wondered at himself for wishing it. He guessed that he was just never satisfied with what he had. That was the way it had been this afternoon, no, yesterday afternoon, when he had been with Beverly. She had laid it on the line with him all the way, and still, when it came right down to it, he hadn't wanted any part of it.

But now he was here, and this was what he wanted before he went home to bed. What the hell, where else was there to go?

And the light snapped on, and she was standing in a door leading into a hall, beckoning silently. He went toward her, still a little unsteady on his feet. She took his hand and led him into a large kitchen.

He sat at a table in the middle of the vast room. A litter of dirty plates and pans stood in the sink, but a place was set before him on the table. Clara sat opposite and held his hand for a moment. She looked old, her hair, red with streaks of grey, hanging to her shoulders, pinless. Shapeless in the large dressing gown. Her lips were stained with ancient lipstick.

"What would you like for breakfast, Kenny?"

"I'm really not too hungry. Beer will do fine."

"How about a couple eggs? I've got plenty."

"Okay," he said, rather than argue.

She turned away, and he decided that if he was going to go through with this thing, he'd have to concentrate on what he had felt, there in the shadows of the other room. Her spirit and her flesh, rather than her outward appearance. And he found that if he fastened his thoughts on those things, the rest of her didn't go too badly either.

Once, as she passed him, he caught hold of her gown and pulled it away from her body, and that, save a certain laxness in the bust line, was something to dream about. The thighs were strong and capable, growing into a pair of large, swelling hips, and he found the darkness of her with his hand, as she leaned and kissed him lightly in passing.

He lit a cigarette and went and stood behind her, as she faced the stove, frying his eggs. Gently, he untied the draw string of her robe, and slipped it off her. She made no move to retrieve it, and she stood passively as his arms stole around her, cupping her, caressing her. Once, she jumped, as the burning fat spit from the pan and scorched her body. He turned her to face him by bringing his hands up to her shoulders and gently pulling.

After he had kissed her again, biting his teeth into her lips, she murmured into his ear.

"Your eggs will burn."

"The hell with them. Where can we go?"

She reached behind her, switching off the gas.

"This way," she said, stepping past him, leaving her robe on the floor. "I'll show you."

He followed her, watching the undulating movement of her buttocks....

She showed him. But he kept thinking of his mother all the time and it left a bad taste in his mouth.

3:30 A.M.

THE SOUNDS crept in around her first. Loud, beating sounds, but she was so lazy and content, curled up in a ball, with her knee tucked up, that for a moment, she couldn't think where she was. It was a trumpet in the next room calling her to get up, but maybe she was still in some sort of a dream, and in a minute, Kenny would be in the room asking her to get up and iron him a shirt for the office. Or to make him breakfast.

Then it was her sense of taste that warned her that she might be in a strange place, her eyes being tight shut against reality and hoping somehow that whatever was trying to tell her something, would go away, and she could drift back into sleep. But the acid kept rising on the back of her tongue, reminding her of the drinks she had had, and from that, her mind progressed to the steak and Cash, and in a rising crescendo, to what she and Cash had done together, not too long before. Slowly, she reached her hand across the bed to where he should be.

But the other half of the pillow was vacant, and immediately, she sat up, with her eyes wide, wondering where he might have gone. It was then that the sounds began to make sense. The music blasting from the record player, and a lot of masculine talk and laughter, and some clinking of ice cubes in glasses. Cash must be having a party, and here she was, in the bedroom, without a stitch on her back. A crimson flood of shame rose to her face. What had she gotten in to? She had heard of things like this happening, but only as a joke. She pulled the sheets up around her shoulders, and listened miserably to the laughter just outside the door.

What had made her go overboard, forgetting all decency, not giving a damn who she gave herself to, ending up in a strange hotel room, with nothing to wear. Her clothes must be somewhere in the apartment. Cash had taken them off in the dark, right there in that next room where the party was going on.

What could she do?

Connie clambered out of the bed and ran to the closet across the room. Luckily, there was a dressing gown, probably Cash's, hanging on the rack. It was miles too long, dragging on the floor, the cuffs swinging loose, below her hands, but it was something to put on. She looked at herself in the mirror. The pins in her hair had come loose and it hung like a black mane below her shoulders. She tried to tuck it up, but it was no use. The hair came tumbling down again.

She crossed the room and stood by the door, listening. Judging from the sound of the voices, they were all men. That was a strange kind of party to have at this hour of the morning.

A faint suggestion of something unpleasant, nibbled at one corner of her mind, but she thrust it back out of sight. She had enough troubles without that.

She heard Cash's voice. It was loud and brash, and you could tell he was bragging.

"... sure was a push-over. She went for the steak routine like a trout snappin' at flies. She was eager to come up to the room. I told you guys I could swing it."

Another voice broke in.

"But how come you took so long callin' us up? We had to leave Mel back in the room. We couldn't wake him up."

"Your old dad had to have a little first, just to see what it was like. You know how it is. I had to test her for you."

Connie's heart seemed to shrink to the size of a pea, as she stood at the door. Her hand gripped the knob like a vise, and she stood rooted to the spot in incredulous silence.

"Where is she now?" she heard another one ask.

Cash was full of answers. Good old Cash. The People's Friend.

"She's in the sack. When Cash is through with 'em, they gotta rest up."

"What about us? How about our share?"

A frightening nausea attacked her stomach, as she stood listening in the dark. It gripped and rolled, and for a moment, she thought she might faint. The dirty men talked about her like she was so much beef on the hoof.

"Give her a chance to rest up a bit. Have some whiskey. She doesn't know about you yet. It'll probably come as a shock."

"This her stuff on the floor, here?"

"Yes," Cash answered. "We were in a little hurry when we got to that stage. Fix some drinks. I'll put her dress and stuff on the bed. Check and see if she's awake yet."

She heard his footsteps coming across the room, and quickly, she leaped into bed, where she pulled the blankets up over the dressing gown she wore. Feigning sleep, passably enough, so that he gave her a quick glance, while he laid her clothing on the bed beside her.

She sighed with relief as he left the room, and as soon as the door shut behind him, she was getting into her panties and bra. The slip and the suit followed, and she heard him explaining to his friends why he hadn't awakened her. Not because, as they thought, he had had his, and didn't care if they got their share or not, but that she would be more willing to give pleasure to five more men, if she was completely slept out and as rested as possible. There was grumbling, but it subsided into a clinking of glasses, and as she slipped her pump onto her foot, it was quiet out in the other room.

Connie peered into the living room. It seemed miles across to the door, and even then, it might be locked. If it was, and she had to face those screaming idiots that lusted after her, she knew she wouldn't have the strength to fight against them, but would just collapse into a quivering, sobbing, heap on the floor. That, of course, would be just what they wanted.

One stop she would have to make on her mad flight across the room. She could see, through the crack in the door, that it lay dumped over, black leather, with the clasp still closed, on the coffee table. The key to Gladys' car was inside the bag.

Evidently, they were all in the kitchen, because she could only see one man in the big room, lounging with his back to her door, facing a doorway just along the wall.

If she could break and run for it, snatching her purse on the way. It would be a toss-up, but she might just do it. She was so panicky at the enormity of the situation, that for a few seconds, she trembled uncontrollably, and it required a conscious steeling of the nerves, before she could muster courage enough to try it.

If the attempt was to be made, Connie told herself, it must be now, before they got impatient again and came in to see if she was awake yet.

She edged the door open another inch. The man she had seen before seemed half doped with liquor. He just leaned on the wall, beyond the door, with his back turned, and kept laughing.

Her feet were like wings, and before she got to the coffee table, she heard the cries of the men, and the pounding of their feet behind her. It was bedlam for an instant, as they boiled out of the narrow kitchen, but she paid them no mind. She couldn't, if her life depended on it.

She snatched at her bag, but it was turned on its side, and she fumbled for it a moment, before her fingers grasped the strap. She had lost a precious split second.

The room seemed endless, as she sprinted for the door. And horror upon horrors, when she twisted the knob, nothing happened. The door stuck.

An instant she tried to force it, and then it flashed across her mind that she had turned it the wrong way, but before she could do anything about it, one of the beasts was upon her, grabbing her shoulder, twisting her around. She was too full of anger at the frustrating doorknob to think of anything but to force it open.

Connie whirled, and instinctively, raised her left knee into his groin with a crushing force. He rolled away from her, and was gone out of her field of vision.

Then Cash was there, grasping at the lapels of her suit and shaking her. She heard her own voice, as though it belonged to someone else, rising in a terrified scream, and she heaved back and away from him with a strength she would never have dreamed possible, and one lapel of her new Christmas suit ripped away in his hand. Grasping the strap of her bag, she swung it fiercely at his head.

It jarred him, a point of one of the buckles jabbing into his eye, and it spouted blood, and he was screaming along with her.

Then, she was back at the door, taking advantage of the momentary confusion in the ranks of Cash's followers. This time she turned it the other way, and the door swung toward her, and she was out of the room and down the stairs, flight after flight of comforting escape.

In Gladys' car, she huddled over the wheel and cried her shame and humiliation out for several minutes, before she was able to take the car out on the road for the long ride home.

As she drove through the deserted streets, a curious rage settled over her. How could she have allowed herself to get into such a position? And it so clearly could have been fatal. She shuddered to think what those drunken fools might have done to her, if she hadn't gotten away.

There was no one to blame but herself. She had asked for it. If she hadn't flown into that silly tantrum with Kenny over that blonde. And now her Christmas present was ruined. One hand fingered the torn lapel.

They had been so happy once. What had happened to them? Kenny had been so distant lately. Surely, she had been all that a wife could be. He had never wanted for anything. They could never say Connie Lawrence was frigid.

Kenny could always have her when they had time for that sort of thing. Only, there was always so much to do. But that was life. Everyone always had so much to do.

But this evening? Did that have to happen? She felt covered with dirt. Not even an hour long, hot shower could wash it away.

Her lovely sharkskin suit. And she knew how much Kenny had had to save to buy it.

As she neared familiar surroundings, the super-market, where she shopped daily, the cleaners that had some of Kenny's clothes this minute, the liquor store, where he got his week-end beer, her heart seemed to leave her body in a mad rush to reach the house ahead of her. She could see the little place in her mind's eye, almost weeping in her desire to get there. Her foot pressed down on the gas pedal, and the car flew swiftly over the pavement.

The street lamps, with their aura of mist and moths, were silent guardians, warning her away from the frivolities of the world, but she saw them not, as she swerved widely into Hidalgo street, pistons and valves humming a joyous tune, and home, home, beautiful, safe, secure, home, just down the block. A lump came to her throat, as she saw Kenny's car parked in the driveway.

She pulled to the curb with a squeal, as the near tire bit into it. Then she was running across the dewy lawn, disregarding the water seeping through her open shoes. Up the front steps of the porch, past the lighted windows, and through the front door.

In that instant, she realized that the business of divorce was not for Ken or herself. Together, they were banded for and against the outside world. It was not too late for them to make their marriage count for something.

She heard the spray of the shower turned up high, and she ran across the room, tossing her purse and coat on the table. They missed and fell to the floor, but she couldn't be bothered. Let them lay.

Her heart was full to overflowing with a great, tender love for Ken, as she entered the bathroom. No matter what he had done, he was hers, and she would fight to the death, before she ever let him go again. Just give her one more chance, and he'd see how she would love him, take care of him. There would be no need to go to another woman ever again, she vowed, and it was like a prayer.

Ken leaned smiling from the shower, kissed her hard upon the mouth, soaking her shoulders and the ends of her hair with his dripping arms. It was a glorious feeling to have him kiss her like that. She didn't even feel the wet. He stood there, like Apollo, with his bright blond hair, damp and stringing across his face, and the bronze of his body gleamed darkly, in contrast to the bleached shower curtain.

Connie felt herself come alive again. Her entire body glowed with an intense desire. She reached her arms around his neck and pulled his head down to hers in another long, breathless kiss.

When they parted, she saw his eyes widen, as he saw the shambles Cash and his friends had made of her new suit. The ripped lapel, the crumpled wrinkles. Not to mention her ruined make-up and her bedraggled hair.

And she was speechless at the sight of his puffed and swollen eye. The poor darling. How had it happened?

Her hand stretched out to soothe the tortured flesh, just as his reached out for her. The two hands met and clasped each other.

"What … how … ?" Ken stammered.

"And you … how … ?" Connie asked.

"Have you had a good look at yourself lately?" A tiny grin started up one side of his face.

"Do you think you're a bargain with that eye?" She tried to hold back, but the laughter came flooding up into her throat, and she could do nothing, but laugh at him and point.

Ken was convulsed with laughter. Clutching the shower curtain, he roared, pointing at Connie. They stood, facing each other, lost in laughter for several minutes, until they could laugh no more.

Connie squeezed his hand, bringing it to her cheek and rubbing it softly.

"We've been a couple of silly ones, haven't we?"

"That's no lie," he said, ruefully.

"Have you been as miserable as I have tonight?"

"Worse."

"I think it would be smart if we kept tonight a secret from each other. I'd rather not know how you got that black eye."

"Same here. I don't care who tore your coat. At least, you got home in one piece."

Connie kissed him again, lingeringly, letting the water drip down the front of the suit. It was a wreck anyway. Might as well finish the job. It was this suit that had started the whole mess.

She smiled at him, adoring his craggy, handsome face.

"Don't use all the hot water, honey. I want a shower before we go to bed."

"I'll be out in a second, darling. I'm starved."

"Want me to whip up some breakfast?"

"Fry me some eggs. Two eggs and some bacon, if we've got any."

"All right, Kenny. You probably need them. Oh, by the way, Merry Christmas."

"That's right. It is. Merry Christmas, honey."

THE END